Tweenage Tearaway

Trixie Tempest

and the Ghost of St Aubergine's

For Jessie and Lola,
who will be tweenage tearaways
in a twinkling

First published in Great Britain by Collins in 2003
Collins is an imprint of HarperCollins**Publishers** Ltd
77-85 Fulham Palace Road, Hammersmith, London W6 8JB

The HarperCollins website address is www.**fire**and**water**.com

1 3 5 7 9 8 6 4 2

Text and illustrations copyright © Ros Asquith 2003
ISBN 0 00 714422 9

Ros Asquith asserts the moral right to be
identified as the author of the work.

Printed and bound in England
By Clays Ltd, St Ives plc

Tweenage Tearaway

Trixie Tempest

and the Ghost of St Aubergine's

by Ros Asquith

Collins

An imprint of HarperCollinsPublishers

Look out for:

Trixie Tempest and the Amazing Talking Dog

Chapter 1

There is a GHOST in my school.

Not your friendly Hogwarts-type ghost, the kind that just pops along to parties with its head under its arm so its mouth is nearer the sausages. Oh no. This one is the real thing. Noises, creepy messages, threats of dire doings, freezing winds in rooms with the windows shut, that kind of stuff. SCAREEE.

I'll take you back to when it first started...

It was a perfectly normal spring evening and I was in the perfectly normal school hall rehearsing for the *Save the World with a Song* concert.

This is a Very Extremely exciting school production we are doing which teaches us all about the environment and saving the planet. It stars Rita Renewable, Goddess of the Future, and Papyrus, God of Recycling. To make it interesting for the audience, Rita Renewable has to fly everywhere on a thin bit of wire; and to make a little joke about Papyrus's Recycling Mission, he has to

go around on a unicycle!

Well, I *think* that's what the unicycle is for, but it could be about Saving the Wheel. In rehearsals so far, we have had to keep stopping while Rita Renewable recovers from crashing into the cardboard rainforest, and Papyrus returns from whizzing off the stage and into the front row of the audience.

So altogether, I'm glad I'm not being either of them, but am a humble musician instead.

I started the trumpet way back when I was eight because seventeen generations of witches on my dad's side of the family have all played an instrument. I haven't got time to tell you about all seventeen generations. But don't cry, maybe I'll do it in another book. My witchy relations are much more interesting than old Henry the Eighth and his wives who we're learning about at school.

I also LIKE playing the trumpet, funnily enough. If you're good enough, you can make it sound like a kind of voice – it's like having two voices to speak in, your own and this bigger, brighter, fiercer one. My trumpet teacher, Danny Vibrato, calls me "The Messenger" because he says I always sound as if I've got something urgent to say.

Anyway, I have to play a big, triumphant, rattle-your-teeth trumpet melody when Rita Renewable first flies on. It's taken me a while to get this trumpet part right, because Danny Vibrato keeps missing my lessons. It's on account of his main job, at the big car factory in our town that looks like it's going down the pan. They're talking about shutting the place down and throwing everybody out of work. I don't like cars because they're Very Extremely bad for the planet, but I feel a bit sorry for Danny Vibrato who's really worried about the factory closing. Because of that, I haven't complained that I've had to find the high notes for the Rita Renewable fanfare all by myself.

Which brings me back to the GHOST...

There I was, practising my trumpet solo in the lonely hall at St Aubergine's Primary.

I was thinking of Danny Vibrato, and how proud of me he'd be that I'd just got it loudly, cleverly, note-perfectly, lip-tinglingly RIGHT, when suddenly I heard it.

Not the trumpet melody, you puddings – of course I heard that – I heard the GHOST!

There was a horrible high-pitched wooooooing moany sound, just like a ghost in a story. And a cold, creepy rush of freezing wind, and all the lights went out, one by one. The moany sound got louder as the hall got darker. The last light flickered on and off as fast as my heart was beating, and the sound turned into a howl, like a wolf. Or maybe a *werewolf.*

I am not a fast runner, but I swear I could've beaten all of Brazil's forward line, the Olympic 100 metre finalists and Spiderman himself at that moment. I was out of there quicker than a cat on fire. Straight out the door at a hundred miles per hour and straight smack-bang into a ghastly, limping, grinning figure. I am sorry to admit that I screamed, very loudly, like in those bad horror movies your parents don't let you watch, but that you smuggle into Stuart Little video covers and take them to sleepovers. (And then wish you hadn't because you don't sleep a wink that night or the next week either.)

My scream surprised Mr Creak, the caretaker,

who turned out to be the ghastly limping grinning figure.

"Patricia!" growled Creak. "Fireworks up yer jumper?"

"No, Mr Creak. Help! There's a ghost in the school hall."

"'Course there's a ghost. There's always ghosts in school halls. Specially schools like this one," said Creak, looking at the horrible plastic and cardboard building that we are forced to go to every day.

If I was a ghost I would go for turrets and spires and stuff, not St Aubergine's. It looks like an oversized egg carton.

"No. Really," I panted. "All the lights went off."

"There ain't no lights on. It's only four o'clock."

He was right. Had I imagined it?

"But it felt cold, and the lights did FLICKER. They DID..." I stammered.

"Too much imagination, Patricia, that's your trouble," said Creak, quite kindly. I think I would quite like him if he didn't call me Patricia.

I felt stupid. But not for long...

I walked home with Dinah Dare-deVille, who'd been late at school too, doing basketball.

"What's up? You're not your usual chatty self," she said, after boring on for half an hour about the latest episode of *Vera the Veggie Vampire*. The radishes had apparently rebelled and driven a steak (I think it was lamb, though it might've been beef) through Vera's uncle's heart, big joke. I don't reckon such a gruesome thing as a steak should ever appear on telly, it will get young people into bad ways.

"Nothing," I muttered, feeling queasy.

"Nothing schmothing. What's up?"

"You'll think it's stupid."

"Go on, tell."

"Promise not to laugh?"

"Swear on the air, swear on the sky, swear on your mother's life. Or I volunteer to die."

I'm not sure where Dinah gets this stuff from,

but at least I could trust her not to laugh.

"Er, well, I've just seen a ghost," I said, not exactly truthfully.

Unfortunately Dinah did not keep her promise. Since she was eating a jumbo ice-cream cone, quite a lot of it splattered over yours truly. But luckily, before I could thwack her with my rucksack, a tiny, ferocious-looking boy cannoned straight into the back of us.

It was Lofty from Year Two (one of the few Infants I can look down on). He was pale as snow and his eyes were all wide and poppy.

"What's up Lofty? You look like you've just seen a ghost."

"I have," he wept. And he charged past us into his house, wailing.

"There. See?" I said to Dinah, with more than a hint of a sneer.

Well, of course we barged up Lofty's path and banged on the door to find out if he'd heard the same things as me, and then what he'd actually seen (horrors!).

But the door was opened one centimetre by a furious-looking woman who said some things that I can't repeat in a children's book, I'm afraid, but they were along the lines of: "Why don't you go away and stop bullying Euripides? You've scared the life out of him. I am fed up of great big young ladies like you pushing

him around and I am going to report you to the head teacher."

I'm sure you can imagine what she said instead of "go away" and "life" and "fed up" and "young ladies". Still, it was interesting to find out that Lofty's real name is actually Euripides. It's amazing what some parents call their children. You ought to be able to report it to Childline, or the European Court of Human Rights, or God, or somebody, and get a refund of a new name.

Dinah finally looked almost convinced. "Trix," she said, a bit more thoughtfully. "What did this Ghost look like?"

"I didn't actually see it," I said, a bit weedily. "I only heard it. But if *you'd* heard it, you'd have run a mile, same as me. It sounded HORRIBLE. Made you think of rusty old clanking chains, tormented expression, horrible twisted mouth, long beard, skull for a head."

"How can a skull have a tormented expression?"

"Skull on its neck, tormented expression on the extra head under its arm," I replied, quickasaflash.

"Shut up," said Dinah, "I really want to know."

"Wailing, moaning, howling, freezing wind,

flickering the lights on and off. Isn't that bad enough?" I said.

"Don't tell anyone else yet," Dinah said. She's always very decisive when anything weird happens.

Well, I told my dog Harpo about it, of course, but she was too busy licking all her puppies one by one, and then licking them again, to pay me any attention. Then I tried to tell Bonzo, my absolute favouritest puppy, but he was having one of those Very Extremely deep puppy naps where you could drop a bomb made of pure Fidoburgers on his head. All he did was wrinkle his nose and snore. So then I had to tell Tomato, because it was Preying On My Mind. This is a phrase of Grandma Clump's: she always says if you have a worry you should not "Bottle Things Up", you should always get whatever is worrying you "Off Your Chest", otherwise it will "Prey On Your Mind". Well, this ghost was on my chest a bit.

Tomato was thrilled, of course.

"Ghost! Wooooo! Shootimded! Getghostbusters."

So me and Tomato played a ghosty game dressed

in sheets, which cheered me up. The puppies joined in.

We were interrupted by a ring on the doorbell. Tomato tottered off to answer it while I tried to unwind myself from the sheet.

"AAAAARGH!"

I heard a horrible scream! Not a ghost at the front door, *surely*?

But yes, of course, Tomato looked very like a small ghost in his sheet, which he had decorated with a lot of dripping red paint and two large black felt-tip eyes. And the scream had come from a trembling woman I'd never seen before, standing next to a man I certainly *had* seen before. It was Danny Vibrato, my trumpet teacher, and I guessed the woman must be his wife.

"Holy Mother of God," she said, crossing herself.

"It's jussagame," said Tomato in his sweetest voice.

"Of course eet ees," said the woman, recovering quickly.

Come to think of it, I remember Danny, who sounds like Jonathan Ross, but has Italian parents, telling me that his wife is the only proper Italian in his house.

"Hello little Messenger," Danny said. "Sowwy the goblins seem to have got in."

"It's just my stupid brother," I said, without thinking. Tomato kicked me as best he could through the sheet, and fell over. I managed to push *him* out of the way and let *them* in.

"Allo Mrs T," said Danny, as Mum appeared from the kitchen. "Sowwy to bother you. I just wondered if we could count on your support about the car works."

"Danny," I interrupted. What I had to tell him would be *much* more interesting, I was sure. "I can do the high notes in the Rita Renewable overture."

"That's tewwific Twix," he said, but I could hear in his voice he wasn't really listening. "I just need to give this to your mum."

He handed a leaflet to Mum. I caught sight of what it said.

SAVE OUR JOBS!
FACTORY TO CLOSE!
Come to the meeting on
Saturday May 10th!
Sign the Petition!

"We won't take up any more of your time tonight," Danny said. "We've still got a lot of houses to visit. But we hope you'll give it a bit of thought. A lot of people wound here, specially at the school you teach in, Mrs Tempest, depend on that car works to put food on their kids' plates." He turned to go. "It's good about that Wita Wenewable solo," he said to me. "You'll have to play it me sometime."

"You can hear it at the concert," I said to him, proudly.

"Ummm, not sure about that," Danny said, rather sadly. "It's the same night as the meeting about saving our jobs. I told my mates there was a clash with your show, but they couldn't change it. Shame it ended up like that. Still..."

He looked at me with a funny look I hadn't seen before. "Maybe it's better to go a bit easy on the enviwonmental stuff anyway. This is a car-making town after all..."

I wasn't sure what he meant by that, but it sounded strange, like he was trying to tell me something without saying it straight out. Then him and Mrs Danny were gone.

"This is very important Trixie," said Mum in her teacher's talking-to-children-as-if-they-were-simple-minded voice. "There are parents at your school and even more at my school who work at the factory. We should support them."

"They're only making cars," I moaned. "There's enough cars in the world. We need a clean environment, which is why we're doing *Save the World with a Song*!"

"Not enough cars!" shouted Tomato. "Want more carslorriestrucks, buses, taxis, trailers, vans, jeeps, coaches, tr—"

"Oh no Trix, what a shame," said Mum, gazing woefully at the revolting sheets.

"Don't worry, Tomato won't mind sleeping in a sheet covered in paint. And the dog wee will wash out," I said comfortingly, in my talking-to-parents-as-if-they-are-idiots-too voice.

But my mother was *not* gazing at the sheets. She was

still gazing at the boring old leaflet.

"It's not that. But it's a *real* problem the factory meeting is on the same day as the concert."

She surely didn't mean it. She surely didn't think a lot of people making dirty old cars were more important than her only daughter?

"Look darling, it's only a school concert. I'm sure they can make it another day. But this meeting is about the livelihoods of half the people in the neighbourhood!"

"And the *Save the World with a Song* concert is about Saving the Entire Planet! And I am doing a trumpet solo when Rita Renewable, Goddess of the Future comes on!" I shouted.

So now I am in the dog house. But unfortunately no dog has joined me as they are all sleeping with Tomato. It's not fair. Even Bonzo has gone off to be with his mum and brothers and sisters.

So I must use my witchy blood from the seventeen generations of witches on my dad's side and think of a witchy plan for:

1. The concert not to be postponed or – horrors! – cancelled because of the rotten old car factory, good riddance to it.

2. The Ghost to leave St Aubergine's.

Of course, I want the concert to go on because it will help Save The World, but I also hope that somebody in the audience will be a talent spotter for Robbie Williams's big band or something, and he will spot my amazing talent at the trumpet and give me loads of gigs so I can add to my MERLIN fund, which is a bit low on account of me getting six comics and a barrel of sweets last week. Anyway, when I have bought Merlin (my palomino stallion what gallops like the wild wind itself, but what I haven't 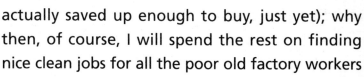 actually saved up enough to buy, just yet); why then, of course, I will spend the rest on finding nice clean jobs for all the poor old factory workers who should never have got jobs building cars in the first place.

I bet Grandma Tempest will be able to use her witchy skills to help me with all this.

Chapter 2

School is even more Very Extremely boring than ever just now, because we are told to shut up all the time because Year Six are revising for the Stupid Exams everybody at school has to do about every five minutes. Mum hates these exams, like most teachers, but they still make kids do them! Why? I think the reason is to make sure children are really worried all the time and therefore realise as soon as possible what life in The Real World is really going to be like. Some

parents get Very Extremely worried too, and lock their kids in dungeons every night and pull their toenails out one by one until they've done at least four hours of homework. These kind of parents keep wagging bony fingers in their children's faces and telling them in scary voices that Real Life is a Big Race and they must come first in everything.

Of course, the good side of this is that the teachers are really stressed out all the time and Very Extremely easy to wind up, as follows:

Year Six are in two classes, and one of them has a high window with a nice wall you can climb on right underneath it, so you can't be seen from inside. So this morning I got up there with Tomato's Punch and Judy puppets and made them have a fight in the window. Pretty soon the whole class were falling out of their chairs laughing and Ms Hedake, who was taking the revision class herself to make them all realise How

Important the Stupid Exams were, couldn't work out what all the fuss was about because I whipped the puppets down every time she looked round.

It seems to me the school needs somebody like me to go round bringing a bit of fun back into life at the moment. They used to have court jesters in the Middle Ages – I reckon they ought to come back; I'd be happy to do that for a job.

Still, there's always the Ghost. That's more interesting than just about anything that's ever happened in our school, and sooner or later the teachers will have to stop and take notice of it, exams or not. In a way, I'm not sure how much I want it to come back, because it's the scariest thing I've ever come across – more scary than the time I ran away from Mum and Dad in the park to Seek My Fame and Fortune when I was two, and then couldn't find them again when I got too hungry to look for Fame and Fortune any more. More scary than the time I fell off the landing window ledge practising climbing Everest, fortunately landing on top of my dad reading the paper in the hammock, which then unfortunately fired us both off like a catapult into the compost heap.

The Ghost is EVEN more scary than the time they made me take a penalty when our all-girl football team played the jeering bald boys from St Herod's school down the road. But since I sent the goalie the wrong way and put it in the top right corner, I reckon I can deal with an old ghost, however scary it thinks it is.

Me and Chloe and Dinah mooched around the school at break, hoping to catch a sign of the Ghost. Nothing doing. So Dinah started doing her teacher impressions. She was just giving Chloe a detention for smiling the wrong kind of smile, when I suddenly realised somebody was listening to us. Somebody with a big toothy smile held together by spots, and a notebook.

"Don't let me stop you," Toothy Smile said when we all started staring at him suspiciously. "It's all good, it's all good."

"Who are you?" we all said at once. "Are you a new teacher?"

"No, definitely not, not at all," said Toothy Smile. "I'm Tony Scribble, from the *Bottomley Guardian*."

(Yes, I do live in Bottomley, and no, I didn't mention it before because I thought you would laugh. My only comfort is that everyone else round here lives in Bottomley too.)

It dimly came back to me that Ms Hedake had said something in assembly about a reporter coming round to do a story on the school, but she was nearly always talking about Stupid Exams in assembly, so I was only about a quarter listening.

"What do you want?" Dinah asked him.

"I want to find out what matters to cool kids your age," Toothy Smile said, while we all pulled about-to-puke faces. "What the hot gossip in the playground is."

"Well," said Dinah, thinking for a bit. "We're looking forward to Food Tech this afternoon. We've had the caretaker's cat on a slow simmer since yesterday and we're going to see if it goes best with chips or a salad."

Toothy Smile's toothy smile disappeared.

"Hey, wait a minute," he said after a bit. "You're winding me up."

"No we're not," I said to him. "But you might be more interested in this. I'm building a nit farm."

The others giggled. Toothy Smile put his notebook away.

"All right, all right," he said, looking around for somebody else to annoy. "You win."

"No, no, it's true," I said, tugging his sleeve and marvelling at my own inventiveness. "I am. My name's Trixie Tempest, and I'm building a place where nits can be happy and not poisoned and scraped and drowned. If we can learn to be kind

to the nit, we can be kind to anything. When I first examined a nit close up, I thought it was the sweetest thing I ever saw. **Nits have a right to peace of mind just like the rest of us.** Everyone's running around trying to save an old car factory where they just make things that poison the air and use up the planet, but I'm going to make something that doesn't harm anybody."

Toothy Smile had taken out his notebook again, and was writing furiously.

"So I'm building a nit farm," I said, "as a first step towards a Better World. And I'm going to show it at the *Save the World with a Song* concert, and play the trumpet, too."

Toothy Smile closed his notebook. He took the camera off his shoulder and pointed it at me.

"You're quite a girl," he said. "Would you mind if I took your picture? It's OK with your head teacher, if it's OK with you."

"OK," I said.

He clicked the camera, and then shook hands.
"Thank you very much," he said, and went away.

"You're a twit, Trixie," Chloe said. "Everyone's going to laugh at you if he puts that in the paper."

"No they won't," I said. "Anyway, he *won't*. He's not really interested in what we think; he really wants stuff about crop tops and boy bands and ear-piercing, and whether we go to football or ballet classes."

"Nit farm," Chloe and Dinah said to each other, giggling as we went back to class.

"Nit farm," I said, as firmly as I could. "I could build one if I wanted to, no problem."

Thinking about nit farms was just beginning to be replaced by thinking about what I might have for lunch when an ear-splitting yell came from the Infants and a whole stream of Reception kids came hurtling along the corridor, burst into our class and hid sobbing under the tables.

This was followed by a furious shout from Ms Hedake.

"How DARE you! Poor Year Six are revising for their exams and you are behaving like, like..." I suppose she was going to say five-year-olds, and then she realised they *were* five-year-olds.

Warty-Beak also saw all this, but had frozen to the spot, so to speak. Like most teachers, he doesn't like children, but Reception children were like a plague of scorpions to him. He tried shouting, but that made them cry more, so then he went all sort of stiff and worried-looking till I almost felt sorry for him.

Mrs Cluck and Mrs Soothe, the two incredibly nice cuddly Reception teachers came bustling in and rounded up the snivelling mob, though not before one had been sick on the Environmental Quilt. "What was all that about?" they asked.

But yours truly had a chill feeling that the Ghost of St Aubergine's had struck again.

At lunch time, the whole school was talking about what had happened in Reception class.

"There was an *eyeball* in the goldfish tank!"

"The play dough made itself into scary shapes and flew about the room!"

"The hamster was found hanging from a noose!"

"I seen Mrs Soothe go purple and her head started spinnin' round and round like a top!"

Lofty was in the middle of a huge crowd of Infants, as he described in detail the ghost he had seen in the Infants' loos the day before.

"It was kind of glowin' an' lurkin'; it was jus a luminous Green Hand, wivout a body nor nuffin', an' it went 'nee-naw-nee-naw', like a police siren.  He looked a lot chirpier, as if seeing a ghost had cheered him up.

Me and Dinah and Chloe went into a huddle. We always go into a huddle when something big happens, but for me and Chloe it was a bit of a scared huddle.

"I've been thinking, since you told me about the Ghost," began Dinah.

"You TOLD her? You've *seen* it?" said Chloe, her eyes on stalks.

"Not exactly." We filled her in.

"Listen," said Dinah. "We don't actually BELIEVE in ghosts, do we?"

"Um," said Chloe.

"Erm," I said.

"You cannot be serious," said Dinah in her Dare-deVille-ish way. "You are grown women of ten, for heaven's sake. This is the kind of story you tell to scare Tomato!"

"Well, lots of grown-ups believe in ghosts," I said defiantly, because I half liked the idea of a school ghost and I half didn't.

"And what else explains it?" said Chloe.

"It's obviously someone doing fiendish tricks," said Dinah. "And I'm going to find out who!"

But Dinah's confidence didn't last long. She and I were on photocopying duty in the office after lunch. This is a really boring thing where you have to get about five hundred letters for parents and carers all stapled and stuffed in envelopes and all, whatever. I think it's dodgy how teachers are always getting us to do this unpaid work but it is better than sitting under the gleaming beak of Warty, specially as we had evil double numeracy skills – that's Maths to you and me. Anyway, we were in the office and the photocopier jammed as per usual. There is a big notice saying **"DO NOT HIT THE PHOTOCOPIER; CALL A MEMBER OF STAFF IF YOU EXPERIENCE DIFFICULTIES."**

So I hit it. And it started shooting out about a zillion sheets. And on the sheets was a message. And this is what it said:

BEWARE the dismal
hand of doom
that lurks within
this very room.
BEWARE the ghastly
hand of green
behind you now
as yet unseen!
Leave this place!
or else, BEWARE!
Make your Escape
or else, DESPAIR!

The Ghost of St Aubergine's was dead, maybe –
but it was also VERY MUCH ALIVE.

Chapter 3

Dinah – cool confident devil-may-care Dinah – had gone a strange shade of primrose.

And still the machine kept spewing out the notes. We belted it really hard and it stopped.

"Well, that was a clever trick," Dinah said. "Who can have done that?" But her voice sounded like someone else's. It sounded like the voice of a very scared person.

Or maybe it was just that my ears were those of a very scared person. Whatever, we were out of the office quicker than you can say WOOOOOOOOO.

We hurtled into Ms Hedake's office.

"Patricia! Dinah! I'm in a meeting!" said Ms Hedake, snapping awake and whisking the pillow from her desk. There was no one else in the room.

"I am just going to a meeting," she corrected herself, and I kidyounot, she blushed. "You know you are not to come in without knocking. Now go outside and knock, please," she added in that velvety voice that meant do this now or I won't be your friend any more. "Do it NOW," she said in a slightly firmer soft voice that made the rubber soles of my trainers go all hot and squashy.

So we went out and knocked on her door and she said, "Come in," and we went in and she said, "I'm just going to a meeting, what do you want?"

Me and Dinah both spoke together very fast. And Ms Hedake said, in a voice that made the windows steam up: "What I just heard was: photocop cop mess pier age be de green ware. Please speak one at a time: Patricia first."

I was struck dumb, because at the exact

moment Ms Hedake turned her steely-soft gaze on me, Dinah fainted.

She came to pretty quick but not before Mrs Balm had bustled in, bundled Dinah in blankets and phoned her mum to come and pick her up. I tried to signal about what had made her faint, but she just looked sort of glazed, as though she had seen a, well...

When I finally dragged Ms Hedake to the office to show her the ghostly messages, they had disappeared. I pressed all the buttons and the photocopier just said, "Out of toner", like it usually does.

"I think you are suffering from imagination overload," said Ms Hedake, in a voice so fiercely hushed that it threatened to scorch the top off the photocopier. "Go back to your class. I shall give a special assembly tomorrow on the Ghost of St Aubergine's, which I have no doubt you will find comforting."

Me and Chloe went straight round to Dinah's after school to see why she fainted. She came bouncing downstairs.

"Why'd you faint?" we shouted.

"Oh. Not 'How are you Dinah? Are you feeling better after your brush with doom?' Just, 'Why'd you faint?'"

"OK. Sorry. Why'd you faint?"

"Oh. I just thought I saw something at the window," she said, pretend casually.

"What did you see?"

"Um, well, a skull, actually."

"A SKULL?"

"Yes. You know, a head made of bone with hollow eyes."

I would've hit her, but she'd only just got better from fainting, so I stood there with my mouth hanging open while Chloe did her motherly bit.

"Oh Dinah. You pooooor thing! How frightful! How ghastly! How absolutely spooky! Have you told your mum? You should see a counsellor," and all, whatever. Chloe doesn't half go on when there's a crisis. Actually she goes on when there isn't one.

"Oh button it, Chloe," said Dinah. "Obviously, I imagined it. What would a skull be doing at the window?"

"What would the photocopier be doing sending ghostly messages? What would an eyeball be doing in the fish tank? Why would a luminous Green Hand be floating around making siren noises at Lofty?" I asked, Very Extremely irritated. What would it take to make Dinah see sense?

"And why would anyone want to hang poor little Hammy?" said Chloe, close to tears.

I felt gutted about poor little Hammy myself, since I remembered his great-grand-hamster, Plum, who had been in Infants when I was a dot.

"Look," said Dinah fiercely, "it IS just a trick. I'm sure of it. We've got to find out who's doing it, but first, we've got to find out WHY. Look for the reason first, then you've got the culprit. OK?"

What is good about Dinah, is she's so positive. Chloe is a kind of half-empty person. You know, you see a glass of chocolate milk shake and Dinah will immediately say it's half full and Chloe will immediately say it's half empty. So I felt a bit encouraged. Surely Dinah was right? I mean, why would a ghost bother to haunt St Aubergine's? It's a mad idea.

Me and Chloe cheered up a bit, mainly because Chloe had a massive marshmallow supply which we munched on the way home.

"I still think there IS a ghost, and you know it's not like me to worry," she said as we got to my house. I sighed. Self-knowledge is not Chloe's Strong Point, as Grandma Clump would say.

"Either way, we're gonna find out. If it's a REAL ghost, we'll bust it. If it's some stupid joker, we'll get him," I said, sounding braver than I felt.

But the sight of Mum's face when I got in was not a pretty one.

"I've had a couple of phone calls about you," she said.

"Oh? Who?" I asked, feeling a bit nervous without knowing why.

"The first was Danny Vibrato."

I breathed a sigh of relief. "Oh, that's all right. What did he want?" I asked.

"He said he's sorry but he hasn't got time to give you any trumpet lessons at the moment," she said.

"That's odd," I said after a bit. "If he's going to be thrown out of work at the car factory he ought to have plenty of time, and need the money too."

"He said there was a bit more to it than that," Mum said. "But he didn't tell me what he meant."

I was going to get Mum to tell me what she thought about this strange stuff from usually nice Danny Vibrato, but she changed the subject.

"The other call was more important," Mum said. "I've just had Ms Hedake on the phone."

"What? What did she say?" I asked nervously.

"She told me there had been some rather strange goings-on and that you and Dinah seemed to be at the heart of it. She said you had pretended there were ghostly messages in the photocopier."

"We didn't pretend!"

"Trix, it's all very well to have a bit of fun, but it's unkind to go around scaring the little ones. Poor Euripides Beaumont's mum has also been bending my ear saying you and Dinah have been scaring him with ghost stories. It's not fair."

"No. It's NOT fair! He SAID he'd *seen* a GHOST."

"Children of that age are very impressionable, Trixie. I expect better behaviour from you, I really do. Now let's not hear any more of this ghost nonsense, please. Go and get on with your homework."

Do you ever find when you're trying to do your homework that lots of other stuff keeps sloshing about in your head and you can't concentrate on the homework for more than about a second? That was happening to me big time. I kept thinking about ghosts and nits and nits and ghosts, and then I got sleepier and they became nhosts and gits, and goats and nists, and after a while gnats and newts, and then they all started scrambling over each other and singing, and eating each other in my head... and... and...

Tomato woke me up by hitting me over the head with a rubber chicken.

"Wake up, Tixie," he said. "It's morning."

WHAAAT? I must have slept about fourteen hours!

"Did I have any tea?" I asked Tomato.

"Um," he said, nodding. "Mum brought tea. Spaghetti hoops."

"Did I actually eat any?" I asked him, examining the rubber chicken, and discovering the yucky information that it had a couple of spaghetti hoops stuck to the hole Tomato had cut in its bottom.

"Um," said Tomato. "Chicken off its food."

Finding I had somehow slept in my T-shirt, I quickly washed and went downstairs to have breakfast with Tomato. We made a frantic dash for the last helping of Krispy Popsickles, as Harpo came bounding in wagging her tail with that morning's paper.

It was the first time she'd fetched the paper since giving birth.

"Clever Harpo! Up and about already and such a good mum too!" I crooned, hoping to get her attention for a moment. But she was off back to her puppies quicker than you could say "woof".

"GOOD HEAVENS! Look at this!" spluttered Dad.

And there, on the front page, which had only a very teeny hole bitten in it, was a Very Extremely big picture of Yours Truly.

There was quite an extremely big headline, too.

"NITS, NOT CARS,"
SAYS TRIXIE TEMPEST

"How on earth did you get on the front page of the *Guardian*?" said Mum, astonished. Well, of course it was the *Bottomley Guardian*. But quite enough people read it around our way to make it about as bad as if it had been in the big posh one.

Dad read it aloud:

"NITS, NOT CARS," SAYS TRIXIE TEMPEST

"Trixie Tempest, of St Aubergine's Primary, South Bottomley, is doing her bit for the environment with a unique project: Saving the Nit. Trixie's plan is to entice all the neighbourhood nits off the heads of local children and into a special 'nit farm', where they can live peacefully.

'When I first examined a nit close up,' said Trixie, 'I thought it was the sweetest thing I ever saw. Nits have a right to peace of mind just like the rest of us. Everyone's running around trying to save an old car factory where they just make things that poison the air and use up the planet, but I'm going to make something that doesn't harm anybody.'

St Aubergine's is one of several local schools involved in the environmental project that is to climax on Saturday May 10th with the *Save the World with a Song* concert. This concert includes many wonderful turns from local children, including Magic from Young Magicians' Circle member Freddy Jones and Acrobatics from the junior Bottomley Athletics Club champions, Roxanne Medley and Samantha Burton.

Trixie's nit-farm project and many others, including a Save the Whale starter kit from Year Four, and a marvellous device made by Year Six to demonstrate the effects of Global Warming (thanks to Mr Skate the Fishmonger, for his donation of ice!) will all be on show before the concert, where Trixie will also be playing the trumpet. Good Luck Trixie! Let's hope there are no nitmares before the show!"

"Well done Trixie," Dad said, drily. "That'll teach you not to talk to the newspapers. Treat it as useful experience for when you become extremely famous. Incidentally, I'm not sure you should have said that stuff about the car factory; it's a bit of a sensitive subject round here."

All this fuss about the car factory! It's enough to make you sick, which is exactly what all those cars smoking and wheezing all over the planet do.

"How you gonna get nits inner farm?" asked Tomato, amazed.

"Um." I had to admit that needed a bit of fine

tuning. But I hadn't yet got over the shock of finding it all in the paper in the first place.

WHY did I always say the first thing that popped into my head? WHY didn't I just do something simple for once, like build a rainforest out of matches, or knit an old Aborigine lady out of recycled newspapers or something. Not that I blame nits for the trouble they cause, not at all. My way of looking at it is, nits have got to behave the way they do to survive. It's "Survival of the Nittest". It's not their fault.

Chapter 4

Ms Hedake's assembly the next day was well attended. Well, assemblies are always well attended, 'cos if you're in school, you have to go. I bet politicians, vicars and such like would love to have such an obedient audience turning up to listen while they drone on and all, whatever. But everyone knew this assembly was about the GHOST and that had everyone quiet as mices, with ears on stalks and so on.

I knew what Ms Hedake would say. I knew she would say we must all calm down and the strange goings-on at the school were all our imagination and so on and on, but I wasn't prepared for the next bit.

"And I must say," said Hedake, after she had said all of the above, "although I have every sympathy with the younger members of the school, who are naturally easily frightened, I am ashamed of the behaviour of some of the older children, in particular Year Five." Here her steely soft eyes swept along the row of Year Fives and stopped, very obviously, at yours truly.

"I will name no names," murmured Hedake, as everyone in the school turned to look at me, "but it seems to me that there are some members of our school community who aren't thinking hard enough about what it means to be part of a community. A joke is all well and good in its place, but when it frightens the youngest among us and disrupts the life of the school, it becomes time to say enough is enough. Certain individuals..."

Again Hedake turned her steely gaze on me "...certain individuals also need a lesson in Citizenship, and not putting their own selfish desires before those of everyone else. It is a great pity that such a stupid prank as this should have been indulged in when the school community needs to be clearly focused on the very important Year Six exams. It leaves me with no alternative in the circumstances but to postpone the *Save the World with a Song* concert until next term, so that the school can concentrate on its most pressing priorities. Those responsible for this unfortunate ghost joke can have time to ponder on the consequences of their actions."

I couldn't believe it. She couldn't have done this. Not possibly. The Year Sixes wouldn't BE here next term! And poor old Freddy Jones had been practising wheelies till all hours and nearly got the hang of his unicycle. But that is typical, isn't it? Exams are more important than the planet! What's the use of a times table if there's nothing left to count?

"GROAN. GRO-o-o-o-a-a-AN. Groan groan groan sigh," went the school. This groaning and sighing was not a ghost. This was every single child groaning. Now if you think that's surprising, you should remember that this was no ordinary concert. We'd been stitching quilts and inventing inventions and rehearsing and working up to it for weeks.

"On a lighter note," continued Hedake, smiling sweetly at the Infants, " I am happy to report that the rumours of Hammy's demise have been greatly exaggerated. He caught his head in a loop of ribbon from the Environmental Quilt, but has made an excellent recovery."

The little kids cheered. Little kids are weird

sometimes. The Infants all ran off, bright as shiny little buttons about Hammy. They seemed to have forgotten the dreadful news that there would not be a concert.

Things got worse after that, if such a thing was possible. Grey Griselda came looming towards me at break with her horrible friends and got me in the Quiet Corner. The Quiet Corner is where you're supposed to go and pretend to read a book or something if you don't feel like playing. I often sit in it with little Billy Clang, who likes reading musical scores. It should be the safest bit of the playground. But if everyone else is playing football it can be a Very Extremely *unsafe* place.

"Little worm here got the concert cancelled," sneered Griselda.

"Oh dear, and no nit farm. What an appalling loss to society," smirked Big Barbara, yanking my bunches. Yulp. I *knew* someone else would've read that stupid article. And it had to be Grey Griselda's gang. Now the nit farm stuff will be all round school and I will be a Laughing Stock.

"Woe woe, no nittys anywhere except in wormy's hair." Big Barbara, who looks about twenty-one and has a pineapple hairdo which makes her even bigger, put her great big face right up close to mine and whispered: "You're dog food now you know. A lot of people were going to show their stuff off in that concert. Now you've ruined it for all of them."

But Grey Griselda said, "My mum says it's a stupid idea, the concert, anyway."

Then she pushed my arm. "Prefer saving nits to paying people to make dirty old cars do you?" she said. "Do you know how many mums and dads make dirty old cars round here? Are you going to be paying those kids their pocket money every week and giving them their tea when their mums and dads aren't able to any more?"

"They bothering you, Trixie?" Phew. It was the *friendly* Year Sixes, Roxanne and Samantha and Freddy Jones. They are really safe and hate bullies.

Barbara and Griselda and their crew swaggered off. "We was just asking if she felt lonely," they lied.

"Hey, love the nit farm idea, how you going to do it?" said Freddy, but nicely.

If only I knew. And if only I knew when I'd get a chance to show it to anyone, now the concert was called off. And if only I knew the answer to whether it was Good or Bad to keep the car factory going, too. Grey Griselda is horrible, but she'd said something that had kind of made my soul itch. Life was getting Very Extremely difficult.

The time had come to write to Grandma Tempest. She doesn't have ordinary things like telephones; she says telepathy works for her and she can't be bothered with machinery of any kind. But I have been *willing* her to get in touch for days, so obviously my witchy blood (what comes from having seventeen generations of witchy relations on my dad's side) is rubbish.

I felt really weird during that break. Some teacher or other seemed to be watching me everywhere I turned, as if I was a criminal. Not that they took any notice when I was getting a hard time from Big Barbara and Grey Griselda.

Then when we all filed in after playtime, I got a cold feeling in my bones. Something weird was happening again.

There were horrible noises from the staff room. Not the usual horrible noises teachers make, moaning about the kids, or crashing cups and saucers and slurping fat bits of cake while we are starving and queuing for the water fountain and all, whatever. But like, horrendous noises! Bloodcurdling screams!

Ms Hedake surged towards the racket, looking

purposeful. "Stay back, children," she ordered. "Obviously nobody thought I was serious this morning. Let me warn you, there'll be exclusions for this, as well as a cancelled concert."

She stopped and looked at me for a second, with one of those looks that goes straight in the front of your head and out the back.

I raised my hands in the air. "I've just been in the playground all break," I said to Ms Hedake. "Ask the teachers."

Hedake turned away and thrust open the staff-room door, with the noise still roaring inside. And do you know, the room was completely empty.

The Hedake looked very pale. Then she looked a bit paler. Then she went paler still. It was like her skin just vanished.

"Look, Miss!" shouted Lofty. "Look! Look! Look!" He was pointing across the corridor into 2B's class. And there, on the board, scrawled in the same ghosty handwriting that the photocopy messages had been in:

BEWARE! The Green Hand of Doom will get you all!
Close the school and run for your lives!

I have got to say here that if I was on a sinking ship I wouldn't mind Hedake being the captain even if she had been horrible up to that moment. She pulled herself together quickasaflash and ordered everyone into the hall.

Mrs Soothe and Mrs Cluck each had to have six snivelling infants on their laps and the rest were queuing for a turn. Then Hedake and the other teachers swarmed round the school doing a search.

When Hedake came back, she looked very stern and called me into her office.

My knees were like blancmange, my head felt as though a road drill was boring through it. To make it worse, my nose was running badly and I didn't have a hanky. Why is it, when you want to be strong and all together and so on, your nose runs and your eyes water and everybody thinks you're crying, but you're not? And I *wasn't*.

"Patricia," said Ms Hedake, offering me a tissue. "I think I owe you an apology." And do you know? My eyes stopped watering, which was weird.

"Clearly you and Dinah were not pretending the other day. Please do apologise to your mother on my behalf and tell her I'll be writing to apologise formally."

"Thanks. What are you going to do about the Ghost?" I asked.

"Oh, I'm sure it's not a ghost, dear. But we'll get to the bottom of it, don't you worry." But Ms

Hedake didn't sound as though she was sure it wasn't a ghost.

"What are you going to do about the concert you cancelled?" I asked next, surprised at myself.

Ms Hedake sighed. She looked as if she was having to think about too many things at once. "I need to think about that," she finally said.

When I came out of Hedake's office, everyone was talking about what the teachers had found: there was ghosty writing on every board in every classroom and all the water in the toilets had turned to green sludge. They were completely blocked.

"Nothing new there then," said Dinah. But I could see even she was beginning to think this wasn't any normal prank.

We all went back to our classes to get notes before home time. Warty-Beak tried to be nice. This was more scary than his usual behaviour as obviously nice is not a word they know on his planet.

"D'you think *he's* the Ghost?" whispered Chloe. "Maybe he's like a vampire, you know, turns into the Ghost without knowing it and wreaks havoc?"

I thought this was certainly possible, but I was beginning to feel certain it was a real, actual, ghost. And I was definitely going off the idea of a real, actual, dead ghost wandering about and going through my school bag and watching me in the loo and all, whatever, like I suppose ghosts do.

"You know, I think Ms Hedake thinks it *is* a real ghost," I said.

"NO!" said Chloe. "Ms Hedake! That's TERRIBLE! If she thinks it's a ghost then we are all doomed."

"Oh lighten up Chloe," said Dinah, not as convincingly as usual.

Sure enough, just as we were all going home with a note to our parents saying we had the next day off school, "Owing to an emergency involving the drains"(!), Dinah gave a whoop of amazement. "She's got the God Squad in! Look!" and she pulled us behind the big oak tree so we could spy on the car that had just zoomed, dangerously scattering Infants, into the teachers' car park.

Dinah's family goes to church every week, so she immediately recognised the vicar's car. We watched while not one vicar, but *two* got out.

"Blimey oh riley! Hedake's called in the exorcist! He's a kind of Ghostbuster from God," hissed Dinah. "Go on Trixie, do your stuff!"

I knew what I had to do.

It is Very Extremely good being as little and thin as me. It means you can hide in all kinds of corners and shadows without people knowing you're there. Sometimes you can spy on the teachers having a quiet smoke. You can always spy on the dinnerladies doing it of course, just by walking up with your plate, because they smoke everywhere, even when they're eating their own dinner. It's a mixture of that and too many bits of dead animal on the plates that made me start packed lunches.

But this was different. This was a Real Emergency and I had to be Trixie Tempest, super-sleuth. Clutching my Grandma Tempest amulet that has been passed down through seventeen generations, I flitted across the school yard, crouched like a shadow behind the double doors, sprang like a cat onto the window ledge of Hedake's office and flattened myself behind the long window box on her windowsill. I could hear all that was said.

"This is Father Befuddle, this kind of thing is more his line than mine," said the vicar. He had gelled hair and a smooth suit, and looked like a children's TV presenter.

Father Befuddle was the Real Thing, though. He was in a sort of wizardy purple robe and had a long white beard and nice witchy eyes, not to boast, but a bit like mine.

"Goodness, Father, do forgive me, I'm sure this is all just some silly prank, but the children are becoming hysterical," said Hedake. "And not just the children, either. Poor Ms Mortice was taken very poorly when she found a severed head in the sand pit."

"A severed head!" gasped the vicar. And I'm glad he did, 'cos I thought I'd imagined it. I nearly fell off my perch, I can tell you.

"Yes. We haven't told the children, of course," said Hedake. "But I'm afraid this has become a matter of urgency."

"But you must call the police immediately,"

squeaked the vicar. "This is murder, or the act of some wicked cult."

I was foxed by this for a minute, but looking at his face I realised he didn't mean what we all mean by "wicked".

"Oh goodness me, no," laughed Hedake. "It wasn't a real severed head. It was a doll! But it was very lifelike," she added quickly, glancing at poor mortified Ms Mortice, the deputy head, who was wrapped in a blanket in the corner of the room and looked as though she wasn't long for this world.

"It is not my experience," said Father Befuddle, "that spirits from the next world, or indeed the *previous* world – they can get mixed up, you know – ever dally with dolls. This sounds more like Black Magic to me. Someone is clearly trying to disrupt this school. Can you think who? Or why?"

But Ms Hedake couldn't think. But I could. I had a sudden flash of realisation as to who would want to and why. I nearly shouted it out there and then, but I wanted to listen to more of the Father. I was dead interested in this idea of a *previous* world.

"On the other hand," said Befuddle, "it could be a poltergeist. They often appear when there are Worried Children of a Certain Age. Are the children in this school worried, especially?"

"Good Heavens, no," said Hedake.

Well, that was a lie for starters. Half of their mums and dads were just about to be thrown out of work, there were Stupid Exams looming and a ghost in the school. But there was something about the way Father Befuddle had said *previous life* and *poltergeist* that had made me freeze to the ledge. My goosebumps were getting goosebumps.

"Well, if you could just do a little exorcism ceremony," said Ms Hedake, "I would be most grateful. I don't believe in it of course," she said, looking through her eyelashes at the vicar, who was a very small bit handsome in a vicary way, "but I gather it works even if you don't believe in it?"

"Over to you, Father," murmured the vicar, backing away from the Hedake, who had gone giggly and girlish.

So then Father Befuddle got out a cross and a thingy of Holy Water and started mumbling chants and prayers and stuff and sprinkling the water everywhere.

Suddenly I felt a horrible stinging pain all down my back and there was a disgusting yowling sound. I screamed and fell off the ledge just as I glimpsed Father Befuddle drop his Holy Water in fright. I fled out of the playground chased by Dinah and Chloe and I ran until I fell in a gibbering heap by the roadside.

"Why'd you do that?" said Dinah furiously when she and Chloe caught up.

"Oh Trixie, you POOOOR thing!" said Chloe. There are times I prefer Dinah and times I prefer Chloe. This was one of those times I preferred Chloe.

I don't want to tell you the next bit, but I guess I have to be honest. The horrible yowling, as Dinah jeeringly explained, was Jasper, the caretaker's cat. Jasper had leapt onto the window ledge as he often does and had been surprised to find he was landing, on all four claws, on a Trixie. That explained the stinging pain.

"Oh," I said.

"So now we'll never know whether the Ghost has been exorcised or not!" said Dinah furiously.

All right then, *she* can climb on window ledges next time. See if I care.

"Oh, so you think there IS a ghost now, do you?"

"Of course not," Dinah muttered, blushing.

"Well, neither do I."

"You don't?"

"I do not. I think it's all a trick and I know who's doing it."

"You KNOW?" Dinah and Chloe were gazing at me with new-found admiration.

"Mmmmmmm," I said, mysteriously.

"Well tell us then."

"I just need a little time to think it through. And work out a plan. And recover from my shock."

"Of course you do, Trixie," said sweet Chloe. "I'm not easily scared, but if that cat had landed on MY back, I would've freaked out COMPLETELY." She glanced witheringly at Dinah.

"If a nit had landed on your back you'd have had to call an ambulance," said Dinah. "Come on Trix," she wheedled. "What's your idea? Who do you think it is?"

"Well..." I said, Very Extremely slowly. "Let's get back to my house first and work out a plan."

So we all went back to my house and it was Very Extremely good fun having Chloe *and* Dinah being so Very Extremely nice to me and stopping at the sweety shop and buying extra marshmallows and Cyanide Schnozzlebursts because they were just bursting to know my Big Idea. This is what it must be like to be the Queen. Devoted slaves doing your bidding and Hanging on your Every Word.

When we got to my house, a horrible sight met our eyes. The kitchen was awash with orange squash and puppies and kids in fancy dress were having a fairy cake battle.

We made a hasty retreat up to my room. Obviously, Tomato had some of his little fiends from nursery school round for tea. My mum does this every few weeks because she thinks she needs to make an effort and give Tomato a social life. She always regrets it later though. She has a dream of nice teas like back in the days before the dawn of time when she was little and children knew words like "please" and "thank you" and "Mrs Tempest". But Tomato's little fiends are not like that.

Me and Dinah and Chloe caught a flying fairy cake each and barricaded ourselves in my room. I was about to reveal the identity of the Ghost of St Aubergine's...

Chapter 5

"So WHO is the Ghost?" Dinah wanted to know.

"Not so fast," I said to her, annoyingly.

"Yes, yes, SO?" she said, annoyed.

"Well, I had a brainwave while I was on the window ledge."

"Yeh, go on."

"It's like in villain stuff on telly, *Crimewatch* and all that. You have to look for a motive," I said, trying to put on a cunning, super-sleuth expression, which I suspected really just looked as if there was something wrong with my eyesight.

"Yes, yes, SO?" they both went.

"I thought, who gains from our concert *not* happening? Who'd prefer it if we didn't have a show about Saving the Planet and cleaning up the environment?" I said, panting a bit for effect.

"Don't know!!!" they both shouted, as if they'd worked out something clever.

"Who'd prefer it if we didn't have a show ON THAT DAY?" I said, even more excited.

"DON'T KNOW!" they shouted, more excited still.

"Haven't you got it yet?" I asked, amazed.

But Dinah and Chloe just gazed at me blankly like two Very Extremely stupid people. Maybe I need to get more intelligent friends. I wonder if you can get them off the Internet?

"The people who work at the factory, of *course*," I said. "Who else?"

"But WHY?" chorused my two little pals.

Maybe I should start treating them kindly, like pets. They obviously have lost the old brain cells they used to have when we were little and had Adventures and such.

"Because the concert is about Saving the Planet, you twits. And to save the planet we don't need cars. Because the Year Sixes have done that big display for the concert showing the world all paved over with roads and how there won't be any trees any more, and everyone will have to walk around covered up even in the summer because there's no ozone layer left to protect us from the sunshine. Do you think those car factory people want everyone around here to see all that when they're trying to get support to keep their stupid mucky old place open? Not only that, but the concert was on the Same Day as their boring old Save the Factory Meeting, and they want lots of people and all the local papers and such to come to THEIR meeting instead. And THAT," I concluded with what I hoped was a modest smile, "is why they have chosen to write everything in GREEN and make the Ghost GREEN. Because they *hate* the environment!"

They **HATE** the Environment!

Chloe flung herself on top of me. "Trixie, you are clever," she said. "You would never know, just talking to you, or from, like, stuff you do at school, how clever you really are."

Oh. Great.

"I don't believe it," said Dinah. "I thought you said you *knew* who had done it. But it's just another of your daft ideas."

"What do you mean? It's a brilliant idea," said faithful Chloe.

"Oh sure," said Dinah. "Well just tell me how they could have done all that without anyone noticing them at school? Even when a new postman comes through the gate Hedake thinks it's going to be one of those blokes who offers sweeties to children; she's on to a stranger in the school like an owl on a mouse. Anyway the car  workers are grown-ups. Grown-ups don't do interesting stuff like ghosts."

"True," said Chloe. "I hadn't thought of that. Oh dear, that means it is a real ghost and I so hoped it wasn't."

For a person who is top at English, Maths *and* Science, Chloe has a surprisingly small brain. I wonder how these things work? I mean, there's me with all these clever wheezes, not to boast or anything, and there's Chloe who can do fractions in her head but can't think her way out of a paper bag.

But I lost the old Tempest temper at that point. Witchy blood started surging.

"They are not coming into the school, you fools," I fumed politely, "they are getting their KIDS to do it!"

"But none of the kids want the concert to be stopped."

"Oh no? Suppose your dad worked at the factory and was telling you you couldn't have Christmas or birthdays any more unless the factory keeps going, what would you do?"

There was a little bit of quiet after this eloquent speech.

Dinah and Chloe seemed to agree I had a point. Me, I was certain of it.

"OK, so we have to find out which kids have folks working at the factory and out of those, who is doing the ghost stuff," said Dinah.

"And I've thought of that, too," I said. "Orange Orson's mum and dad both work there. And they must be horrible, 'cos he's horrible and they let him smoke which means they would hate environmental stuff and all that and he is always trying to get money for fags."

"Yes!" said Dinah, coming to life at last. "Orson it must be! But he can't do it all by himself."

"I don't want to sound wimpy, you know, I do want you to be right," added Chloe, cautious as ever, "but I do think you shouldn't jump to conclusions about who is the Ghost. Orson is innocent until proved guilty."

Huh. Orson is about as innocent as Darth Vader.

"Oh shut up, Chloe," said me and Dinah, happy-as-larry now we had a PLAN.

At that exact moment we heard frightened shrieks and Tomato burst through the door in a storm of kids and puppies. They were not a pleasant sight as they seemed to have been rolling in ketchup and possibly egg mayonnaise.

"Look Tixie, look, look! Ghosty!" shouted Tomato, waving a green bit of paper.

"Oh no!" I groaned, recognising the ghosty handwriting. "They're after ME now."

I grabbed it and read:

"YOU may set your priests upon me
But they will not make me go.
Either close your school for ever
Or face a lifetime's woe.
THE GREEN HAND IS COMING CLOSER..."

Argh! "Where did you get this, Tom-Tom?" I said.

At first it was impossible to hear him above the general din. Some of the little kids were making "wooo-wooo" noises and waving their arms about. One was wearing a pillow case and putting on a weird howling noise that sounded as if he had earache, which became a real howling noise when a door handle turned up at exactly the same level as his nose seemed to be. Some were crying, some were telling each other to shut up; one or two were lying on the floor with their thumbs in their mouths; a couple were swinging plastic hatchets around their heads, which sent a bunch of flowers in what was fortunately a plastic vase sailing over the banisters on to the fluffy head of a slow-moving Harpo, who was innocently heading into the now empty kitchen in search of leftovers.

But eventually I was able to hear what Tomato was saying to me.

"Ghosty bought it. Hahaha shootimded."

Eventually we pieced it together. Apparently there had been a strange noise, like a fire-engine's siren – just like the one Lofty had heard in school. The kids had all rushed to the door and seen a green hand coming through the letter box with the note.

"Didn't you open the door?"

"No. We was scared," said a tough-looking kid dressed as Batman, going puce and bursting into a torrent of tears. It was like watching a small blushing fountain.

Then the bell started ringing as all Tomato's little fiends' mums and dads and carers came to pick them up.

Batman and co trooped off as my mum muttered to herself, "Thank you for hosting the infant lunatics' conference this year, Mrs Tempest. Oh no, no trouble at all..."

Me and Dinah and Chloe grabbed a barrel of biscuits for comfort and ran back upstairs.

"Look, how did they know I knew about them?" I asked, shakily.

"They're probably putting it through all the doors of kids at the school," said Dinah.

"Well let's find out," I said.

"It's getting dark, and it's going to rain," said Chloe nervously. And it was true. It was only five p.m. but there was a humungous cloud hanging over our street. "Anyway, I promised Mum I'd go home 'cos she's taking me up to the fancy-dress shop to get stuff for my costume for the concert..." She stopped.

We all looked down at the floor.

"Oh," Chloe said. "Of course there isn't a concert now." Then she brightened up. "My mum'll probably take me anyway, to make it better," said Chloe. "If she does, why don't you come too, and forget all this ghost stuff?"

I was tempted. But one look at Dinah changed my mind.

"Oh pooey," said Dinah, as Chloe abandoned us. "Let's go get the phantom postman."

"Shootimded," said Tomato cheerfully.

And so it happened that me and Dinah discovered a Most Interesting Thing.

As we were heading for Lofty's house, thinking he would be certain to get a leaflet, I saw somebody in the street I was just about to shout "hi" to. Then I suddenly froze. It was Danny Vibrato, my nice trumpet teacher. But he was with a group of very tough-looking men.

"Shhhhh! Duck down! Look!" I hissed.

We hid behind the hedge and watched.

"That's Danny, my trumpet teacher. His real job is at the car factory. Those men must be from there too. Maybe they're going into that house for a meeting. Perhaps they'll talk about how they made the Ghost wreck our concert."

As usual, tiny Trixie was the one who had to go and do the Daring Spy Stuff.

I slunk like a shadow into the porch and pressed

my ear to the lighted window where Danny and his mates had all sat down with beers. But I couldn't hear them. I knew I'd have to take my life in my hands and break in.

Clutching Grandma Tempest's lucky amulet, I crept like a mouse round to the side gate, flitted like a cat off the roof of the garden shed and up the water pipe, and slid like an eel into a half-open window.

My heart was thumping like hearts are supposed to in books. I couldn't believe I was braveasalion. But I was. I landed on feathery feet and slid, quiet as a cloud, down the banister.

I could hear voices, including Danny's, coming from the front room. Danny was saying: "We have to stick together and follow this thwough to the end, whatever happens. There's no turning back now. We've got them in a corner and they're getting hurt, and we have to keep the pwessure up."

Horrors! He was talking about our school and the Ghost! How could he have done this to me? And what were they planning to do next that was Even Worse?

There was a big cupboard right next to the door. If I got into it, I could be even closer without the danger of being seen.

I opened the cupboard door and climbed in amongst a lot of musty old coats and hats. I could hear the men even more clearly now, agreeing with what Danny was saying. The monsters!

Suddenly a cold, clammy, wet-feeling thing landed on my head, and slipped down around my neck. I fell out of the cupboard into the light. Aaaargh! This was to be the end of Trixie! It was... it...was... a luminous GREEN HAND!!!!!

It was all I could do not to scream a horrible scream. Instead, I made a squelching, gaspy sound, which is what a horrible scream sounds like when you are trying not to make it.

Hardly knowing what I was doing, I flapped at the horrible hand around my neck like a duck flapping its wings, and amazingly knocked it back into the cupboard, when I banged the door shut behind it.

"What's that?" said a voice from the room.

I crouched low, ready to fly out the front door like an arrow. I was mesmerised by the Green

Hand. I thought it would wake up and fly out of the cupboard and strangle me all by itself.

"Oh, just the cat," came another voice. They must have some strange cat. But I could hear footsteps coming towards the hall. At that moment I would've rather been caught by the Factory Men than by the Green Hand. But now that I knew it was a real ghost, and not a trick, I thought, maybe the Factory Men were in league with the Devil Hisself, and had harnessed the Forces of the Dark Side to help them in their Evil Plot!

Just as the footsteps got to the door, I leapt up out of my frozen state and hid at the side of the cupboard. One of the men just poked his head round the door, gazed around and went back in, saying there was no one there!

So now I was trapped. If I tried to go through the front door, the men would hear me. If I went back upstairs, the Hand might batter its way out of the cupboard and come and grab me! I crouched completely still, my hand gripping the cupboard door handle tight, terrified it would start to turn, for what seemed an eternity. The hairs on the back of my neck were getting little hairs on the backs of their necks. I tried to listen to the voices in the front room. But I could only catch a few stray words: "meeting", "strike", "politics", "wages" and other boring grown-up words like that. Then I heard, "ghost of St Aubergine's" and everyone laughed!

I realised like I never had before that these ordinary-looking men were a Dark Army from an Underworld of devilish fires and sulphurous smoke and all that. Even Danny, who had been like an uncle to me!

Then the doorbell rang.

One of the men came past me to the door. It's just as well I can make myself look very small, and I'm small enough to start with. The side of the wardrobe was at an angle where neither of them could see me.

"My little brother kicked his football over your house. Can I have it back please?" I heard Dinah ask in her most *charming* voice.

"He ought to be in the England squad then, mate," said the Factory Man, admiringly. "That'd be a free kick from about fifteen metres out."

He went out into the back garden to find the ball. How normal these devils could make themselves seem! He'd walked right past me again, while I was shaking like a leaf in a gale! But I had made myself as tiny and witchily small as it's possible to be. As soon as I heard him open the *back* door, I shot out of the *front* door, like a cheetah, into the street.

"What took you so long?" asked Dinah, turning crossly to me.

Not, "Oh, I was so worried, I thought you'd been eaten by a mad axe man," but, "What took you so long?" I wished and wished I had gone off to the fancy-dress shop with Chloe.

"Well, come on, did you discover anything?"

"I saw the Ghost," I said simply. "It's the same ghost as Tom-Tom saw. It's just a luminous green arm, on its own, with a horrible skinny, slimy, *clammy* hand with long fingernails. It could murder you as soon as look at you. Except it hasn't got any eyes. But it doesn't need them. The fingers just go where there's... where there's... living flesh."

We screamed.

"We've got to call a meeting of the whole school," said Dinah, when we'd finished screaming. "If everyone phones two people tonight, we can get loads of kids to come. We can all get to school an hour early and meet in the playground. If adults won't solve this problem, we will!"

Then the rain started. First the humungous cloud let down a few big fat heavy drops, then it burst and it was like having a bucket of water poured straight over your head. We ran home.

Now I am trying to work out what to do. I can't tell any adults I'd seen a real ghost in a stranger's house. They will think I am a burglar, or mad, and lock me up. But I cannot sleep.

I shall have to write to Grandma Tempest, this very minute.

Dear Grandma Tempest,

Thanks for the amulet sorry I never wrote before. Can you help please we have a ghost in our school. I URGENTLY need the following:

SPELL TO GET RID OF GHOST.

I would be very grateful if you could also send me a idea how to make a nit farm and that witchy trumpet book you said Great Aunt Zarabeena had. If this is all too much please concentrate on the ghost which is urgent.

Your affectionate granddaughter

Trixie

(Tobias's daughter, Tomato's sister)

You may think that last bit's a bit funny, but witchy families are very big and also vague and Grandma Tempest has, I think, sixty-two grandchildren and four more on the way. (Of course, I couldn't fit them all on the family tree in my last book, 'cos the pages weren't big enough.) There are times I prefer Grandma Clump – at least I am the Apple of Her Eye.

Chapter 6

Well, I phoned two people and Dinah phoned two people and each of those others were supposed to phone two people, and each of *them* were supposed to phone two people and so on and on, but of course they didn't. Or maybe it was the rain that had gone on pouring all night and was still coming down as though it was the rainy season in a monsoon forest or something. So the Great Children's Meeting held before school was a bit small. Seven of us to be eggzact: Dinah, Chloe, Sasha the Skate, Lofty, Bugsy, Wax, and me.

The Secretive Seven

Sasha-the-Skate   Bugsy   Wax   chloe   Dinah

ME

Lofty

"Seven's a good witchy number," said Dinah, positive as ever. "Tell them what you saw, Trix."

So I told them. I did exaggerate a little bit and Lofty looked tearful.

"You mean the hand actually *grabbed* your throat?" said Chloe, eyes like footballs.

"Not exactly," I admitted.

"But you did see it move?" she persisted.

I thought about this for a minute. "Well... not exactly."

"You mean you didn't see it move? At all?"

I went a bit quiet. Well, very quiet. I was beginning to have that rather stupid feeling you get when something is not quite how you thought it was.

"Did it look at all like THIS?" said Chloe, pulling something from her school bag.

We all shrieked. It was the Luminous Green Hand.

"They've got loads at the fancy-dress shop," said Chloe, pleased with the effect. "Enough to haunt all the schools in England. They've done it very well, it's got some kind of slimy-feeling stuff on it, so it feels pretty alive."

You know when you get helpless giggles? You know, the kind of giggles that start as just a little snuffly, squeezy kind of hiccup, far away in a distant labyrinth somewhere near your tummy. Then they start racing through all your tubes and pipes, getting faster and faster, making a kind of naaaaaaaahhhhhhhmmmm noise that gets louder and louder, until you feel whatever bit of your brain is supposed to be in charge of you is bouncing helplessly up and down on the end of them, like a cork on a fountain of water? Then, just as, say, the head teacher is trying to tell you some very sad story about starving old people in a desert or something, they hurtle out of your nose and mouth like those scenes in *Titanic* where doors break and the sea bursts through.

Well, we got those sort of giggles. But in my case, there was an alarm bell ringing in the background of my giggles. It was ringing with a very sad little message that said, "Brrrrrrring Brrrrring! Stupidity Alert! You, Trixie Tempest, are a Very Extremely stupid person. You have just won the Stupendously Stupid trophy, that entitles you to wear a T-shirt for the next hundred years with the slogan, 'I am amazingly daft' on it."

Eventually everyone's giggles ground to a halt, even Lofty's, although we had to bang him Very Extremely hard on the back and jiggle him about a bit.

"But hang on," said Dinah. "This proves Trixie was right!"

Eh? What?

"It IS the factory people! The Green Hand was in their house! What would they be doing with one of those? They must be the culprits!"

The little alarm bell in my head turned into a nice jingly bird song which said, "Tweety chirrup, tweety chirrup, you, Trixie Tempest, are a Very Extremely clever person. Tweety chirrup, tweety chirrup. You get to wear the Cleverclogs Person of the Year T-shirt."

"We'll have to tell Ms Hedake," said Chloe, folding the grisly green arm back into her bag. But at that point Grey Griselda, bang on time for school, came zooming over, took poor Chloe by the collar and frog-marched her towards the Hedake's office.

"You'll have some explaining to do, Chloe Caution," said Griselda nastily. "You've been caught green-handed."

Of course, I rugby-tackled Griselda to save my friend and of course, Warty-Beak was striding towards us at that very moment with his infra-red laser eyes boring into me.

"Patricia! Let go of Griselda this instant!"

I held on like a limpet.

"Griselda's attacking Chloe!" shouted Dinah and Sasha.

But you know how it is at schools. Griselda is in Year Six. She has fairies on her lunch box and ribbons in her plaits and always sucks up to teachers and they all think she is a nice person. Whereas she is in fact a Very Extremely horrible person who makes Warty himself look like the tooth fairy.

"Nonsense," cackled Warty, "she is clearly defending herself from this dervish. Let go at once, Patricia!"

And I am ashamed to say I let go, but that was partly because Griselda stamped very hard on my foot without Warty-Beak seeing it. It was the sort of thing that makes you think how difficult a football referee's job is.

"Patricia and Dinah, come with me this instant!" said Warty.

"But why?" said Dinah defiantly.

"You have already been cautioned, I believe, for picking on Euripides. But to shake him so hard like that is bullying!"

Warty-Beak *does* have infra-red eyes. He must've seen us from right over in the teachers' car park.

"No. It wasn't like that," said Lofty, bravely. "And p-please don't use my real name in the playground!" he begged, pathetically.

But Warty wasn't listening. He marched us to Ms Mortice's room, while Griselda dragged Chloe towards the Hedake.

So much for the Great Children's Meeting!

And so now me and Dinah are in detention and Chloe has been suspended! Poor old good old kind old Chloe, of all people. The Hedake, who is usually a reasonable person, for a head teacher, has gone ballisticus. She called the whole school in for a special assembly and said she had found the culprit and that the Ghost of St Aubergine's would no longer be roaming the ancient corridors and all this. Then she made Chloe stand in front of the Whole School.

Poor Chloe stood there with her lip trembling, being smirked at by Griselda and Orson and their gangs. It is disgusting, like Victorian Times, and Freddy Jones stood up and said so. And the

Hedake shouted so loud at him that poor old Freddy sat down with his head in his hands, which meant he must've been crying and he is nearly twelve!

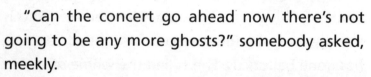

"Chloe will be suspended for the remainder of term," continued the Hedake, "and anyone who dares to say another word on this subject will meet the same fate."

"Can the concert go ahead now there's not going to be any more ghosts?" somebody asked, meekly.

"Of course not!" the Hedake thundered. "I was beginning to think I had misjudged you all when it seemed as if the noises and strange phenomena might actually be due to some natural cause – a fault in the plumbing or something similar—"

A lot of people looked at each other with raised eyebrows.

"—but now that my worst fears are confirmed and this disagreeable prank is indeed the work of a misguided pupil or pupils, my original decision stands. It pains me to say it, but the concert is certainly suspended for this term."

Nobody said a word. Me, I don't care about the concert any more, or the stupid nit farm or anything. I am going to save Chloe from this terrible smear on her character if it is the last thing I do. Charity Begins At Home as Grandma Clump says. Chloe's my friend. If I put planning to save nits, however deserving, 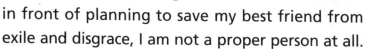 in front of planning to save my best friend from exile and disgrace, I am not a proper person at all.

That very same evening, I got home and there was a long purple envelope for me from Scotland. Grandma Tempest! Why do nice things happen too late to do any good? Still, I was dead impressed with this super-express witchy postal service. Maybe they do use owls? I ran upstairs and barricaded my door against Tomato.

You never know, I thought, she is psychic and a witch after all, so she may know everything that has happened.

But no. Her letter, written on silver paper in purple ink with all splodges, went as follows:

Dear Grand Daughter Number 30,

Enclosed: One spell for removing Ghosts from Primary Schools.

One spell for removing Ghosts from Secondary Schools.

If you are still in Primary, the second one will come in useful later no doubt. It will stay fresh for ten years as long as you can find new toad's spit and enough midsummer's day dew.

Also enclosed: BEWITCHED, BOTHERED and BEWILDERED, Jazz Melodies for Trumpet. Be sure to learn a tune a day. Your Great Aunt Zarabeena mastered the book in a week, but with Clump blood in your veins, dear, you will be considerably slower.

Also enclosed: PLANNE FOR NITTE FARME devised by my Grand Mother's Great-great-great-great-great-Uncle Xarabon. He used it

with success during the Wars of the Roses, when the soldiers were much plagued by these creatures. There is no new idea under the sun, my child, but you may pretend the idea is yours. His spelling may be a trifle hard for you, though I know children are no longer taught proper spelling as we were, but rest assured, "NITTE" is nit, "WOODE" is wood, "YE" is either "you" or "the" and so on...

Affectionate regards to Tobias – and to his dreary wife. Oh, I'm sorry my dear, I suppose she is your mother!

Must fly.

Eugenia Tempest (High Priestess of Egg)

I looked at the two little black and gold parcels and the trumpet book and a very ancient scroll entitled PLANNE FOR YE NITTE FARME – all too late to do any good but I was too upset to even open them and chucked the

lot in the bin. So much for witchy blood and telepathy. I have a granny who doesn't even know my name! When I had signed the letter with it, and everything!

But I had more important things to do than worry about that. I had to go and see the Factory Men and get them to come clean about the Ghost, so Chloe can be proved to be innocent. Maybe even Hedake would see sense then, and agree to put the concert back on.

Mum sent me to bed early, which was just fine by me. I stuffed a pillow under the covers to make it look like I was asleep and as soon as darkness fell I climbed out the window and slid down the drainpipe and ran like the wind to the Factory Man's house. Yes! The lights were on.

I didn't think, I just charged straight up the path and banged on the door like a loony.

And he appeared. It was the same man who went to fetch the football, but he was bigger than before. He had all bristly hair and big bulgy muscles that could've squeezed the life out of me.

I suddenly felt very cold and wobbly.

"Er..." I said.

"Yes?" he said, looking at me as though I was a cold and wobbly thing that he might just fancy biting in half to see if it was refreshing.

"Nothing. Wrong house." And I ran into the dark.

"Hey," he shouted.

My heart was thumping like a drum 'n' bass record and my breathing was creaking like a rusty bike. I forgot all about Chloe. I forgot all about everything but running. But then I heard other footsteps running too – much heavier footsteps. HIS footsteps!

"Oy!" he was shouting. "Come back here!"

Then I could hear what seemed like an army running after me, all shouting! Oh no! Why hadn't I bought Dinah? Stupidly, I turned into the park. I was running in a park after dark with a horde of mad strangers chasing me! Was I, in fact, as stark raving bonkeroonies, off my trolley and fit for the funny farm as you probly thought I was right at the beginning of this story?

Then I did what people always do in films when they are being chased through dark tangly undergrowth by mad axemen. I tripped over. When I'm watching those films I always think, don't go there, I wouldn't do that, look where you're going you fool and all, whatever. But let me tell you, when you are scared out of your wits *in real life*, then this is the kind of stupid thing you do. As I fell, spraining my wrist, a voice came into my head. It was the voice of the friendly policeman, PC Toecap, who had talked to our class the previous week about Health and Safety. PC Toecap's voice-in-my-head said: "SCREAM VERY LOUD", so I did.

But the only other sound in the universe was

Factory Man and his gang, crashing through the undergrowth. He was nearly upon me!

Suddenly there was a ferocious yapping noise and a tiny furry cannonball launched itself at Factory Man's throat.

BONZO!

Factory Man lurched to a halt and grabbed my pet! He was going to strangle my beloved Bonzo!

"LEAVE HIM ALONE!" I shouted with all my might, hoping against hope that PC Toecap, or even Warty-Beak, or anyone, would come to

Bonzo's rescue. "LEAVE HIM ALONE!" I shouted even louder, but what actually came out of my little dry throat sounded like an ant sneezing.

"Don't worry, he won't hurt me," said Factory Man.

I blinked.

The blurry monster who was attacking Bonzo came slowly into focus. Bonzo was treacherously wagging his tail and licking Factory Man's face from nose to chin. And Factory Man was *stroking* him.

"Well, he's small, but he packs a punch," said Factory Man. "Good to have him on your side."

"Don't touch him," I said – I wasn't sure whether I was saying it to the Factory Man, who I was beginning to be in two minds about, or to Bonzo.

"Well, he doesn't seem to mind," said Factory Man. "But it's you I'm worried about. Aren't you a bit young to be out on your own so late?"

I always forget I look about six.

"I think we'd better get you home."

"My mother told me not to go with strangers,"
I said fiercely. I backed away from him, holding my
fists up defiantly, and fell into a duck pond.

But Factory Man had obviously called his entire
household out to chase me, because a nice woman
who turned out to be Mrs Factory Man and her
nice teenage daughter fished me out, made a lot

of fuss of me and took me and Bonzo back to their house, where they wrapped me in a blanket, made me hot choccy and asked for my number so they could phone my mum. Er, no thanks, I would rather've been eaten by eels just that minute, or ducks, which I nearly was.

"We don't have a phone," I said convincingly. "We're travellers," I added.

Mrs Factory Man warmed my heart by giving Bonzo a whole dish of Fidoburgers.

"They're his favourites!" I said, and then wondered if maybe travellers don't give their dogs Fidoburgers, which are in fact disgustingly expensive as my poor mother is constantly pointing out.

"Well, your mum and dad will be really worried about you, so you must tell us where they are," said Mrs Factory Man kindly.

"Oh, I'm a orphan traveller," I said, thinking if I could just get them out of my hair for a second I could make a run for it. Although I knew that tearing Bonzo away from the Fidoburgers was going to be tough, I asked to go to the loo and amazingly, Bonzo came too!

Once I was in, I slammed the loo door shut and locked it. There were all kinds of photographs on the walls, quite different from the postcards from Spain, prints from art galleries and old copies of Cheerio! magazine we have in ours. One was of a lot of people carrying a banner saying, "Don't Lock Us Out Of The Future", whatever that meant. And one had Danny Vibrato in it, playing his trumpet in front of the factory, with a lot of people laughing and looking surprisingly nice. But I soon got distracted by Bonzo, who was leaping up and down making it pretty clear he liked me a lot better than a Fidoburger, which was a big surprise.

I stuffed Bonzo into my pocket like a twitching handkerchief, and pushed open the Very Extremely small loo window. I was just able to squeeze through, and when I got out on to the ledge I

pulled Bonzo from my pocket, expecting to see him squashed flat like one of those animals in a TV cartoon. But he looked as round as ever, and so pleased to see me again (must be nice being a dog, the same thing can be a surprise to them about every two seconds) that he leapt out of my hands with excitement and hung in space for a moment, pedalling his almost invisible little legs. Then he shot downwards past the window ledge with an even more surprised look on his face. I made a grab for him with my good hand and a grab for the window frame with my sprained one, and

neither of them grabbed anything so I followed Bonzo out into petrifying empty space.

I hoped the fall was going to be like Alice in Wonderland falling after the White Rabbit, and that we'd go very slowly past all sorts of interesting stuff on shelves, and land very softly in a wonderful world without all the horrible frightening things going on in this one.

We did land softly, fortunately, in Factory Man's rather smelly compost heap. Mr and Mrs Factory Man were standing there, looking down at us. Mr Factory Man picked us up and brushed off a few potato peelings and squashed tomatoes. A small green frog jumped out of one of my pockets and hopped off. Must have been from the duck pond. "Wondered where you'd got to, you little monkey," he said to me. "Thought you might try to run for it."

"I don't think you are an orphan traveller, are you dear?" asked Mrs Factory Man very sweetly. "In fact, I think I've seen you at St Aubergine's Primary."

I don't know how I looked more familiar covered in compost than I had on her sofa, but I would prefer not to think about that.

So anyhow we went back inside and that's how I finally told them what I'd come about, although by this time I didn't believe they were the sort of people to pretend they were ghosts and go round frightening little children. And the more I told them about the Ghost and how I was sure it was people from the factory, the sillier I felt.

"But what makes you think it was us?" asked Mrs Factory Man, and although her voice was kind, she was looking at me as though she thought I should be in a home for Very Extremely stupid persons.

"I... I don't think it was YOU," I said, "I think it was your friends, you know, who came round for the meeting."

Whoops. How would I know that?

"How would you know about that?" asked Mrs Factory Man, with what I think was a twinkle in her eye.

So then, although I hated to do it, I confessed about climbing up their drainpipe into their window and seeing the Luminous Green Hand lurking in their cupboard about to strike me dead and strangle me to boot. "Although of course now I know it was not lurking, but sort of hanging in there," I blushed. "But it must've been left there by your friends, and now my best friend is in big trouble and everybody's blaming her for getting the *Save the World with a Song* concert cancelled and her name is mud. And so on..." I trailed to a halt. After all, why should Mr and Mrs Factory Man care about the *Save the World with a Song* concert or my friend anyway? They were probly going to lose their jobs and their house and their cupboard and their drainpipe and their compost heap and everything.

But my confession had a Very Extremely surprising effect that surprised even me.

"**Freddy!**" shouted Mrs and Mr Factory Man.

I trembled and tried to shrink into a corner. What monster was this Freddy going to turn out to be?

And then, to my great surprise, a sheepish-looking boy shuffled in: Freddy Jones!

"Hi Trixie," he grinned, shuffling from one foot to the other.

"Freddy! Is this your house?" I asked, not a very intelligent question if I'd thought about it a bit.

"Freddy, Trixie here has been telling us a lot of very interesting things..."

"I know. I was listening at the door."

"Bit of a coincidence isn't it, you being so good at magic and conjuring tricks, and all?"

This was true, now I came to think of it. Freddy was often showing off magic tricks at school; he was completely amazing at them.

"Have YOU been doing all this ghost stuff?" his Dad asked him.

"Erm. Yes." Freddy shuffled from foot to foot again. I remembered him trying to speak up in assembly and then crying and I hoped he wasn't going to do it again.

His mum went over and put an arm round him. It didn't look as if either of his parents were going to get mad. They suddenly seemed real stars.

"Were you thinking of us?" she asked him. "Were you thinking all that Save the Planet stuff was going to stop anybody caring about whether the factory got closed down or not? Were you thinking more people would come and support us if the school show didn't happen on the same day as the meeting?" She squeezed him. "It was wrong of you to do all that; it must have frightened a lot of the little kids. But it's great you were doing it to help us."

Freddy was silent for a minute, and sniffed. "Actually... I wasn't," he finally said.

"What d'you mean, you *wasn't*?" his parents asked him together. "You mean you didn't do it? Did you do it, or didn't you?"

"I did do it... but it wasn't about your meeting, or the factory or anything."

"Then why?"

"Me and some friends started it, as a joke, to get out of..."

"Get out of WHAT?"

"The Stupid Exams. We thought it would disrupt the school so much that we wouldn't have to take them. We had all kinds of other stuff lined up, setting off the fire sprinklers to spray green water, putting blood-coloured glop in the

soap dispensers, lowering
severed heads from the
ceilings—"

"WHAAAT?"
everybody said at once.

"—not real ones, papier
maché ones of course. It
was all coordinated together
like a firework display. There's
an amazing kid I know..." He
trailed off.

"What amazing kid?" I asked Freddy.

"Well I'd better not say," Freddy mumbled.
"Don't want to get anybody else into trouble. But
it's someone who helped me with a lot of it. His
dad runs the big Guy Fawkes' display for the
Council. He knows how to organise all this stuff.
Still, I suppose it sort of... got out of, um... hand.
Sorry." Freddy blushed deeply. "I am sorry, I really
am. I was going to own up tomorrow to save
Chloe," he added.

And I believed him, I really did.

I looked at his folks worriedly. Most mums and
dads would've gone ballisticus at this point.

But Freddy's parents were Very Extremely nice.

"But Freddy, why are you so scared of the exams? You're a clever boy!" said Freddy's mum.

"It's not about being clever," said Freddy. "Samantha and Roxanne are dead clever at Gymnastics! And Sasha is great on a skateboard! And Bugsy is brilliant at Art! And Trixie here is a wicked trumpeter! And I'm... dead clever at Magic! But none of us is going to be tested on any of that!"

"Well, the schools can't test everything," said Freddy's mum kindly.

"NO. But the tests are nothing to do with what I enjoy doing. I like writing stories but the English test is about counting adverbs, whatever they are. Roxanne writes fantastic stories but she is going to fail her English because she takes about five hours to write one. The exams don't give you time to THINK!"

Freddy put his head in his hands and really did look about to cry this time. He looked at me. "It's all right for you, Trixie," he finally said. "You're the kind of person who doesn't mind all this. You come from the sort of house of people who don't mind exams. You've got friends who are good at them; your mum's even a teacher herself. I wish I was at St Herod's where cool kids like Tommy Vibrato are; down there nobody expects much and you can just do the stuff you enjoy."

"Oh dear. Perhaps we've spent too much time worrying about the factory and not enough listening to you," said Freddy's dad. "We'll have to talk to the head teacher and apologise, of course," he added.

I tugged at Mr Jones's sleeve. "Tell Ms Hedake that Freddy did it because he's worried about failing his exams, she'll understand," I said breathlessly. "She'll know then it wasn't just us being naughty and trying to make trouble. She might let us go ahead with the concert then. Please!"

He looked doubtful. "Not sure how much of an effect somebody like me will have on her," he said after a while. "But we'll certainly try."

Then they all walked me home.

On the way they told me some things I hadn't realised before. Like Grey Griselda's mum being the boss of the factory, who had been trying to get them all to work harder for longer hours and less money for years, and was finally telling them all to get lost. Like how Freddy's parents, and Danny Vibrato and some others had found a company willing to buy the factory and keep all the workers on to experiment with alternative fuels that are nicer to the environment but that Grey Griselda's mum and her bosses wouldn't listen. About how they suspected Grey Griselda's mum had even been trying to get Hedake to stop the *Save the World with a Song* concert because of the anti-car stuff in it, long before the Ghost first appeared – maybe even threatening not to give the school the money her company was paying towards a new Science room unless she agreed.

I got back home very late, my head spinning with so many thoughts. My mum was horrified at first to find I'd got out of bed to go running around the streets, but when Mr and Mrs Jones told her what had happened, and how *me* trying to clear Chloe's name had accidentally allowed *them* to find out what was troubling poor Freddy, she just made me promise never to do it again and left it at that. She even came to tuck me in when the others had gone, something she hadn't done for a while.

"You're a good girl, Trix," she eventually said, stroking my head. Bonzo crawled into my pile of clothes on the floor and walked round in circles, wagging his tail.

"Do you think Ms Hedake will forgive Chloe and agree to the concert going ahead now Freddy's mum and dad are going to explain everything?" I asked her.

"I don't know, dear," Mum said. "But we're all going to do everything we can to make her."

I was just thinking about how nice it was to have Mum on my side when I fell asleep faster than about any time in my life ever before.

Chapter 7

HOORAY!

Hoorah, hooree, humungous hoorays and hooreenies!

Chloe and her parents have had an apology from Hedake, and the concert is reprieved! Mr and Mrs Jones and my mum, and quite a few other parents went to talk to Ms Hedake about exam stress and how sorry Freddy was and all, whatever, and she's changed her mind. She changed it pretty slowly, according to Mum, but when they were telling her about Freddy, Mum said she swore there was a tear in Hedake's eye. My witchy blood *told* me there's some good in her. The only person who isn't over the moon about this looks like Grey Griselda, who seems to be under instructions from her mum to go round telling everybody what a dumb idea it is. But now that the concert has been moved to an hour earlier, and the Factory meeting has been moved to an hour later, the workers at the Factory are going to have their own stall at the show, showing people the alternative energy stuff they could be getting into if they were given a chance.

But meanwhile I was fretting about Grandma Tempest's black and gold packages. I wanted to get the secondary school ghost potion (just in case), and most of all the trumpet book and the nit farm design!

Now the concert was going ahead, I had to practise my trumpet like a loonytic (especially since Freddy had noticed I could play...) AND I had to make a nit farm quickasaflash. The bloke from the *Bottomley Guardian* was bound to be there, and I was going to show him I'm not a Trixie to be trifled with.

But of course I had binned it all in a fit of Tempestuous temper! And my adored mother had put out the rubbish bags. And the dustmen were due early next morning. So I propped my eyelids open with matchsticks, and at midnight when the world was snoozing, Bonzo and me yawned our way out to the bins and went through every bag. Bonzo enjoyed this more than me. It's horrible what one family throws away each day. But yes! Under several tons of old cartons and tins and bottles and peel and stuff, I found the soaking parcels. I took the two little packets, "Ghost Primary" and "Ghost Secondary" and stuffed them in my dressing-gown pocket. I stuffed the trumpet book in my trumpet case to look at later, though I couldn't help noticing it said "High Magick Grade Twelve" on the corner, and was obviously going to be far too hard for me.

But the best thing was the nit farm plan as follows:

PLANNE FOR YE NITTE FARME

Made this daye bye mye hande and under mye seal – Xarabon Nebuchadnezar Wagnitude, Warlock of ye Outer Hebrides, Inner Hebrides and Hackney marshes.

First must ye build ye box out of finest woode. Let it be foure cubits this way and a few cubits in ye other direction. Let it be painted in blues and greenes and varnished with the spitte of toades. Let it be filled with ye lockes of hair from ye lads and lasses and dames and damsels and yokels and lordships of ye lande. Be sure to finde ye haire that be flaxen and ye haire that be darken. Ye haire that be springy and ye haire that be silken. May ye haire be from ye heades of ye many and not of ye few!

When ye lockes are laide within ye boxe, be sure to weave and plait them into a cosy neste so that ye nitte will be happy within.

Then write a signe on ye boxe such as wille be pleasing to ye nitte: such as, "WELCOME Ye NITTES of ye worlde, maye ye finde rest withine these walls."

Then shall ye request each afflicted soldier, or parson, or peasant, or king, to place his heade close unto ye boxe, so that his lockes will blend with ye lockes within. Then shall ye nitte runne happily from ye haire of ye afflicted unto ye haire cosily woven and plaited within ye boxe. And there live a long and happye life, afflicting no live personne, but going about his dailye business among his own kinde.

Which I reckon meant: make a box of some size or other, (a few cubits here or there wouldn't make much difference) paint it blueish, varnish it (I am NOT going to get toads' spit so don't ask) and get your mates to give a few hairs to put in. Then, anyone who has nits can put their heads in the box and the nits will jump off their hair and live happily ever after in the nit farm! Cool! And I will get a little magnifier so people can watch the nits all happily playing on little nit swings, and all whatever. Phew.

So then I got an old shoe box (OK, not wood, but Time is of the Essence, as Grandma Clump would say), sloshed some of Benjy's blue and

green powder paint over it, varnished it with my tweenage nail-varnish pack (Supa-dupa-nailtastic) which made it go an interesting purply colour (I did add a bit of duckweed as I bet it's got toads' spit in it) and made a cute little notice board:

WELCOME TO THE Nitz

******

FABULOUS SIX STAR NIT HOTEL...
Hair mattresses on every bed! Hair shirts under every pillow! Blonde breakfasts! Bunch Brunches! Ringlets with plaits for lunch! Mohican with braids on sideburns for tea! Fringe benefits include: Dreadlock Suprise Nightcap, Curly Cocktails and, for dieters, Skinhead Slimmer Squash! Every kind of hair you've ever dreamed of! Nit lotion—free zone!

Then I scissored a bit of hair off the snoring Tomato, added a bit of my own wig, decided against using Harpo's hair on the grounds it wasn't a flea farm, fell into bed and slept like a twig.

Next day, when I got to school, the hall had been transformed for the *Save the World with a Song* concert. Old Creak and Mortice and Hedake must've been up all night. Even Warty-Beak had a jolly green hat on, which was not a very nice sight, making him look like a praying mantis eating a greenfly on the next branch up, but at least he tried. The *Save the World* 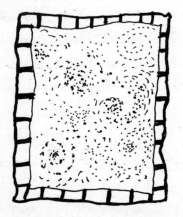 *with a Quilt* quilt looked Very Extremely nice I must say. I was quite glad my little square, which was of nits dancing but turned out looking a bit like what happens when you splatter ink off a toothbrush, was quite near the top and since the quilt was hanging from the ceiling, it was almost invisible.

Grey Griselda's square, all elves recycling milk bottle tops, had been the best, but fortunately her mum had made her change it at the last minute into one about a smiling jolly family dancing round their smiling jolly little yellow car surrounded by trees and flowers and sunshine. It had been a bit too much even for Grey Griselda to get it together in the time and bits were still hanging off. So

they'd put it even higher up on the quilt than mine. Yah boo to her then.

Everybody was dressed in green except about three quarters of the school who didn't have anything green and they were being done up in long green sheets by poor Ms Mortice. She was still looking a bit green herself as it happens, but it may've been because she had been up all hours dyeing the sheets. I wished I had've gone for a sheet myself instead of scrabbling around at the last minute for some green clothes. I had ended up with my dad's fishing wellies, some old green tights of my mum's and one of Tomato's T-shirts with "SAVE THE SNAIL" on it. Oh well, such is life.

There were stalls everywhere selling home-made cakes, sweeties, drinks and all, whatever, as well as a lot of "crafts" made by the Infants out of pasta and loo rolls. I suppose the Infants' mums and dads will buy them: "Ooh look.

Another lovely pasta and loo roll sculpture to join the other 234 we've got already, how nice."

I spent the next hour gathering hair for my nit farm. Everyone was very obliging, although I admit I had to creep up on a few scaredy-cats with my shears. Soon the box was well full and I set up the notice and charged 5p a head for people to come and stick their heads in the box so the nits would jump off their hair and into the nice cosy **Nitz HOteL.**

All the mums and dads began pouring into the hall about four o'clock and started spending their dosh. Year Four did fantastically with their Save the Whale Starter's Pack which very cleverly had little model whales made of papier maché moulded round a water pistol. You could squeeze the hidden trigger when showing it to a teacher or somebody's dad and hit them in the eye, claiming it was all in the interests of showing people how whales work.

Year Five had made a machine that showed what would happen if there was no ozone layer left at all. It was a bit gruesome, with models of people on beaches all shrivelled into crisps and turned into skellingtons, and one person was actually supposed to be alight, which I thought was going a bit far. But they were selling loads of Halloween Masks to show how our skins will all melt and fall off and stuff if we don't save the Ozone Layer, which were very popular with the Infants who were running around in them letting off bloodcurdling screams.

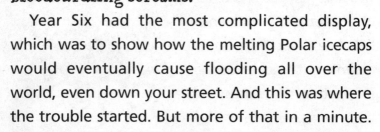

Year Six had the most complicated display, which was to show how the melting Polar icecaps would eventually cause flooding all over the world, even down your street. And this was where the trouble started. But more of that in a minute.

I wandered over to the Car Factory stall where Mr and Mrs Jones, Freddy, Danny Vibrato and a few of the others from the factory were showing off some very pretty working models of how in the future we might run cars off water, chicken poo, methane gas and all kinds of strange stuff to do with chemistry that I couldn't make out. Danny tried to explain some of it, then spotted my trumpet in its case, slung over my shoulder.

"Make sure you have a warm-up before you play it," he reminded me. "Weckon you've got it all sorted?"

"No problem, Danny," I said to him. "I've been practising a lot."

"Do the nits like it?" he asked me.

"I think so," I said, after thinking a bit. "They seem to run around a bit faster, maybe they're dancing."

"I'm sowwy I stopped your lessons," Danny whispered to me so nobody else could hear him. "It was all getting a bit difficult. We just didn't think anybody at this school cared what we were on about. But it's all turned out for the best, and I just hope we can save the

Factowy in the end. You want to keep the lessons going?"

"Of course," I said. "I want to get into the Youth Orchestra next term."

"And you will, too," Danny said.

Feeling much happier about everything, I went to look at the Year Six amazing icecaps thingy. The Year Sixes had really thought of everything. There was a huge block of ice in the middle of the display – provided by Mr Skate, the fishmonger – which was kept frozen by some electrical machine, watched over by Year Six brainiacs with glasses and little white coats. Little model villages were scattered about all over a lovely landscape made of felt, and though a few Warhammer figures hacking each other and a model Gandalf standing at a bus stop seemed a bit out of place, it all looked pretty amazing, with real water rivers sloshing round it adapted by Mrs Green from the Bottomley Garden Centre using the bits from an ornamental pond.

"It's all a bit over the top, don't you think?" said one of those loud shaddup-I'm-talking grown-up voices that sounds like somebody blowing a trombone in a library. I turned round to see who it was. **Aaargh! Grey Griselda's mum! What was she doing here?** It was like the Devil turning up in an RE class. And she was talking to Ms Hedake, who was looking a bit uncomfortable standing next to her.

"I think it's wonderful," Hedake said, just as trombone-like so everybody could hear her.

Ms Mortice was running around the room like a battery toy, gathering up performers. "It's time for the concert, Patricia, get on the stage," she muttered, as she whirred past me. She tripped over an electrical cable on the way and almost fell headfirst into Year Six's very realistic-looking Amazon River (though I couldn't work out why Captain Hook's pirate galleon was sailing down it), avoiding it only by plunging her arm, unfortunately in its nice neatly-ironed white sleeve, into the dirty brown water to support herself. I helped her up while she clucked and squawked like a chicken, and tried to free her arm that was caught up in a little chain under the water. In the end, I pulled hard and she came free, with a big plop from the River Amazon.

I ran for the stage with my trumpet. The Year Six brainiacs were looking worriedly at their machine and shouting questions at me, but I didn't have time to stop.

We all got on the stage, elbowing each other, and when we lined up there wasn't room for Bill Clang, a tiny boy from Year Four who had to bang two cymbals together bigger than him.

So he fell off the back of the stage trying to squeeze in, taking most of the back row with him with a huge crash like a lot of people falling on top of a greenhouse. Quite a lot of people's instruments got muddled up in this accident. When they got up again the flute player had a triangle, the triangle player a bass drum, and one or two people no instrument at all, so they started practising humming roughly the way they thought it ought to sound.

But I was sweating all through. I had to do a good trumpet solo in the finale, which would be the moment for me to come on as the Pied Piper, to draw all the wood spirits and animals towards me.

And so, as the little Infants dressed as squirrels and woodlice and mushrooms and wood sprites and all, whatever, streamed on to listen to my beautiful solo, I walked proudly on stage, raised my trumpet to my lips, and caught sight of Danny Vibrato who came to the front and gave me a thumbs-up. There seemed to be a lot of noise coming from around the Year Six icecaps display, and people running about with buckets, but I closed my eyes and just concentrated on the trumpet. Some of the prettiest notes I'd ever played came out, all in the right order, without any growls or burps or splutters, and the little squirrels and woodlice and mushrooms all started dancing about in a circle.

But there was something Very Extremely

funny about seeing woodlice and mushrooms dancing about, and I felt a terrible, big laugh rising up inside me, trying to get out of the trumpet.

I got to the biggest, toppest note of my beautiful trumpet solo... then let out a huge snuffling, snorting, shouting GUFFAW like a donkey that's just thrown somebody over a hedge. Everyone started laughing. But then I noticed something disastrous happening to the Year Six icecaps. I could see that a lot of brown water was washing about all over the floor as if a flood had come in. Horrors! I must have pulled the plug out of the Amazon River when I was helping Mortice free her hand from the murky waters. Mr Skate's big block of ice, which appeared to be melting fast, slid off the table on to the floor and whizzed across the room like a huge ice-hockey puck.

Water was now gushing all over the hall from the icecaps exhibit, which had of course become an even more realistic picture of the effect of Global Warming on our Planet than Year Six had ever intended. Teachers, and the Year Six Brainiacs were running around in circles trying to find out how to turn the water off, but Mrs Green from the Garden Centre, who'd set it all up, was talking very busily to Chloe's mum in a corner – Chloe's mum is the biggest Gardening Lunatic in the Entire World –

and didn't hear any of the hysterical calls for her to report to the icecaps display as soon as possible.

Back on stage, Mortice had quickly recovered from guilty feelings about accidentally setting all this stuff off, and jumped about in front of us all, shouting, **"THE SHOW MUST GO ON!"**

I thought it was like the band playing on the *Titanic* really, but I was up for it if everybody else was. Bill Clang said "Yes" by banging his cymbals together with as much force as possible, making us all jump out of our skins.

We had completely forgotten about Rita Renewable, Goddess of the Future, who had been curled up on a platform high up at the back of the set, and was – as usual – painting her fingernails and reading a teen magazine called *Luv-Bytes*, not caring that much about The Planet one way or the other. At the brain-splattering crash of Bill Clang's cymbals, which was her cue, she leapt up and pulled the release that allowed her to float on the wire, goddess-like, across the stage, scattering flakes of green fairy dust all around her. But she came on upside down, still clutching the teen magazine, and dropped the bottle of nail-varnish on Mortice's head, creating a horrible Monster-Mask expression as the red liquid dripped in axe-murderer fashion down the side of poor Mortice's face.

Rita Renewable proved that when the going got tough, she had the Star Quality that had allowed her to demand the main part until everybody else surrendered exhausted. She waved pics of pop star Alvin Pose and soap-queen Sharon Thong in full view of what was left of the audience, then squeaked from her upside-down position:

"Come Fairy Sprites and Woodland Elves,
Think not only of yourselves!
Come little flowers from elfin dells,
Come goats and sheep and ring your bells."

I blew a big loud long note on the trumpet as a way of saying "Yesssss!" to Rita Renewable. She smiled in satisfaction at A Job Well Done and she swung back across the stage, hit a horrified Mortice, and knocked her like a bowling-pin into the front row, straight into the startled arms of Warty-Beak. His horrid visage changed from greenish-grey to pale-ish pink. Phew! I thought, nothing can get worse than this, but as you will have often noticed in this story, dear reader, Trixie Tempest was WRONG AGAIN.

Papyrus, the Tireless Recycler, then grabbed his moment to star, by rocketing on in full Unicycling

Glory. I was Very Extremely impressed, because unlike all the rehearsals, Freddy Jones didn't shoot off into the front row of the audience before he'd had time to say a line of his speech. He kept whirling and doubling back around the stage as if he was happier on wheels than walking. People started cheering and clapping, which considering the chaos going on all around the hall by now, was pretty impressive, I thought.

Rita Renewable must've felt the audience was getting into Freddy's corner, and she didn't want to let him get away with anything just because he'd got lucky once and not fallenoff. Disentangling herself from what remained of the rainforest, she swung upside down back across the stage, shouting out like an announcement on a railway station before Freddy could get a word out:

"Come join your hands, repel the foe.
Together we have far to go,
To build a world that's fresh and clean,
And unpolluted – EVERGEEN!"

Look, I want to break off for a minute and promise you that I didn't write this stuff. It was written by poor old Mortice, I think after the severed head experience, so you have to make allowances...

Anyway, back to the concert and Ms Hedake, who decided to get a grip on things now that the whole event seemed to be turning into a lot of people running around with buckets, squeaking daft poetry upside down, discovering they were better unicyclists than they'd ever thought possible, and all, whatever. Freddy had just brought himself to a standstill and was about to say something or another, when Hedake yelled out, in a voice everybody could hear, whatever they were doing: "LADIES AND GENTLEMEN,

STUDENTS, PARENTS AND GUESTS!"

There was a silence, broken only by the sound of water still running from the Year Six icecaps exhibit.

"I want to tell you that there is something you all can do, this very day, to help save not just the planet, but your very own children!" boomed Hedake.

There was a hush all round the hall.

"Most of you may know that this school has recently been haunted by a ghost! This ghost was the work, not of Chloe Caution, who was, I am ashamed to say, unjustly punished for it, but of many hands... I will name no names, because those involved have been honest with me – but without endorsing their decision to take these actions, I have reconsidered a number of things I had previously taken for granted.

"They took these actions, misguidedly perhaps, but forgivably, to let us know of their dissatisfaction at an examination system that labelled them 'clever' or 'stupid' before they had a chance to find out who they were; before they had had a chance to learn about this wonderful planet

154

we live on, and how we are all equals in our duty to help sustain its future for these children, and their children, and their children's children."

There was a huge cheer. A tall man I hadn't seen before, took a picture of Hedake in front of the stage, nodding enthusiastically as she spoke. I thought she caught his eye before she went on. Hedake smiled, a strange creaky, ziggy-zag smile you hardly ever saw, but reminded me of how she had looked at the vicar.

"To explain these matters further, please join me in welcoming our friends from the Car Factory, who have come here with ideas that can turn our dreams of a more sustainable world into a reality."

At a big round of applause, Danny Vibrato and Mr and Mrs Jones stepped towards the microphone. But before they could say anything, there was a cry of:

"Rubbish," from a long pointy woman in

the audience, still wiping cream tea off the front of her blouse.

It was Grey Griselda's mum! "This show is a disgrace! This is supposed to be a school, not a soap box," she screamed.

There was a horrified silence. What would Hedake do? But before she could move, Mr Jones took the microphone...

"Hello, St Aubergine's," he said, in a friendly way, as if he was talking to us all one by one. "Thanks for thinking of us."

A big cheer drowned out the squawkings from Grey Griselda's mum.

"I have a very important message for everybody here today..." Mr Jones went on. "The world cannot survive unless we completely change our ways about renewable energy, and about RECYCLING!"

Freddy Jones heard this Magic Word spoken in

his dad's big no-denial voice, and leapt back on the unicycle. "I am Papyrus, God of Recycling," he shouted, pedalling furiously. But, proving that unicycles are definitely *not* the transport solution of the Future, he bumped over the edge of the stage. Freddy took off over the handlebars of the unicycle, and his poor head collided – THUNK! – with the fire alarm panic buttons that say **"Any Pupil Improperly Activating The Alarm System Will Be Subject to the Most Severe Punishment"**.

Slinging my trumpet behind me, I ran towards poor Freddy as he slid down the wall, whimpering slightly. Mr Jones stopped talking and ran towards him too.

A horrible, whining, whooping alarm sound began to whirl around the hall.

The fire sprinklers started up, spraying HORRIBLE GREEN LIQUID over everyone.

A massive cloth dropped down behind the stage, showing huge pictures of Ghosts Dripping Bludde and eating poor innocent children, and the sound of horrible cackling laughter replaced the noise of the alarm. Big flapping bats on wires snaked down from the ceiling and

started squirting red liquid over the screaming Infants, who tried to clutch on to the legs of their screaming parents, who thought they were crazed goblins and tried to whack them off. I reached the groaning Freddy Jones just before Mr Jones did.

"Freddy, Freddy, are you all right?" I squeaked.

"Am I alive?" Freddy asked me.

"It looks like it," I said to him.

"Good, I'm probably all right then," he informed me, relieved.

"Freddy, what is all this?" I panted. "You told us all about the Ghost, I thought it was over, what's happening?"

"It must be Eight Brains Eric," Freddy gasped. "He was the one helping me do all the ghost stuff. The one whose dad organises the firework display on the common. He's a genius at making weird stuff all go off at once. He set this stuff up last week. Good isn't it?"

"Good? It's ruining the whole show! Why didn't you tell him the ghost stuff was all over?"

"I couldn't. He got chickenpox two days ago and hasn't been able to come out of his house. I thought it would be OK because he said all the stuff wouldn't go off unless he activated the system, but something must have gone wrong."

"I'll say it has," I said sadly, as the ghostly noises died away, the twitching bats from the ceiling stopped twitching, and the huge cloth behind the stage just started to look like a lot of not very good pictures of daft-looking, badly-painted ghosties rather than a Message From The Dark Side.

Mr Jones took Freddy's hand, picked him up, and took him down the side of the stage into the audience without saying another word.

Ms Hedake took the microphone and very quietly spoke to those who were still capable of listening to her rather than quivering with fear, squeezing brown water out of their trouser-legs, wiping red goo out of their hair and all, whatever.

"May I apologise on behalf of St Aubergine's, friends and guests. Unforeseen events have, sadly, spoilt our evening of celebration. Rest assured you will be receiving an explanation and an apology. Goodnight."

She left the stage without looking at anybody. The tall man I had noticed earlier was pushing his way through the parents trying to rescue their lost, soaked, green or fake bludde-spattered children, to reach Hedake, and he looked as if he had something important to say.

But I didn't want to listen to anybody else saying anything else to anyone. I didn't even look for Tomato, or for Mum and Dad. I ran as fast as my legs would carry me out of the hall. I passed Mr Jones, clutching a sniffing Freddy to his chest, and the way he looked at me in silence made me forget everything else. I bumped into Danny Vibrato at the door, who just shook his head. "It's nobody's fault, Little Messenger," he

said to me. "It's just Fate. Maybe we're not meant to Save The Planet. Maybe the Factowy isn't meant to survive."

Chapter 8

Well all right, I stayed the night at Chloe's. At least it was one stroke of Very Extremely good luck that I'd already fixed up to do that 'cos Mum and Dad had planned on going to the Car Factory Workers' Meeting after the show. I did not fancy being at home with Tomato and the baby-sitter (because the baby-sitter is always Very Extremely nice to Tomato and Very Extremely ignoring of me). That gave me one whole night to think of a WAY OUT.

Chloe, as usual, failed to look on the bright side.

"Now I'll be excluded for ever and ever and ever," she wailed, as if going to school was the best fun she ever had.

"No you won't. Freddy and his parents will have told them what happened, and it worked before. It wasn't Freddy's fault, how could he have known Eight Brains Eric would get sick and not be able to call off the ghost stuff?"

"But look what else happened! Icecaps melting! More bats and ghoulies disrupting the show!"

I admit it looked bad. Very bad. And it wasn't even our fault.

But it got worse.

The very next morning at 8.30 a.m. a Very Extremely unpleasant thing happened.

Chloe's doorbell rang and there was my mum, fuming like only a Very Extremely fuming mum can fume.

"This was delivered, by hand, it must have been very early this morning. Can you explain it?" she said in an icy tone that made me feel icy. And she thrust a letter into my hand and this is what it said.

ST AUBERGINE'S PRIMARY SCHOOL, BOTTOMLEY

Dear Parents/Carers of Patricia Tempest,

As you are no doubt aware, today the school concert and environmental fair were severely disrupted by some of the pupils. Your daughter, unfortunately, has already been proved to be one of the ringleaders.

As a result of the scale of damage and disruption caused, I have taken the unprecedented step of delivering this letter by hand.

We expect you to bring Patricia in at 8 a.m. on Monday morning to have a meeting with myself, her form teacher, Mr Wartover, and the chair of governors about her behaviour. At present, unless she has a satisfactory explanation of the events, I can see no option but to exclude her. Needless to say, I have written to the parents of the other culprits in a similar vein.

Yours faithfully,

Araminta Hedake

Head teacher.

I screwed the letter up and threw it on the floor in despair. "We tried to do everything we could to Save the World," I wailed to my mum. "It wasn't our fault things went wrong. It wasn't our fault the Stupid Exams make kids like Freddy so unhappy he started doing all the stuff him and Eric did with the Ghost. Grown-ups are so UNFAIR! Nobody bothers to think about it from our side."

Mum marched me home and I fell into bed. I don't know if it was because of getting very wet in the polar icecap, but I was not feeling that great.

Later Mum came in and sat down and handed me another envelope. "This one's from Tomato," she said. "An extremely wet kiss came with it which I won't pass on. He said this was a Very Special Present for you."

He had made me a card. Yes, OK, it had pasta stuck on it and something that had probably been knitting wool in another life, but he had also written, in his very best writing:

I never cry as you know, but I had to wipe something out of my eye after that.

"Tomato," I said to myself, as if he was standing there. "You are the best brother I've got."

Of course, next day I woke up at first bird song (well, it was the merry rattle of the milk van) and the dread of doom came flooding back. I could not speak until we got to Hedake's office and I felt even worse because Dad had put on a suit, which I have only ever seen him do for a funeral.

The only words I could think of were, "I'm sorry but I didn't mean it." And I knew they would cut no ice with Hedake.

But at the first sight of the Hedake, the Warty-Beak, the School Governor AND the Mortice, even these words froze on my lips. Because all of them were, look, you won't believe this, but ALL of them were SMILING.

How could they? How COULD they smile at my pain?! They were just like those children who

162

watched poor Chloe being beheaded and executed and so on and then went away all happy and full of beans the very next minute. But these were grown-ups. And teachers!

"We're awfully sorry for all the trouble Trixie has caused," blurted Mum. "And she is very sorry too, aren't you?" She gave me a little shove, but I couldn't speak. The sight of Warty-Beak's gleaming rows of fangs twisted into something so like a smile had completely drained me of any courage I'd had left.

And then the Hedake rose up, her eyes gleaming like a gorgon.

"Mr and Mrs Tempest, Patricia, thank you for coming. There have been significant new developments since I wrote to you. Do sit down."

And so we sat down with a thump. Oh no. New developments. There was something even worse to come. What else had happened? Maybe I wasn't just going to be excluded. Maybe I was going to be expelled.

The Hedake ploughed on.

Oh, great, I thought. I am about to be put in front of a firing squad.

But then everything was OK.

Everyone had said it was a great show! About three quarters of the parents had said they were in agreement about the Stupid Exams, and how they stopped their children from doing anything interesting.

THEN a large number of parents had gone off to the Car Factory Meeting and met all the parents who worked there and they had all phoned up the other parents and they had got a big campaign started!

"But the most important thing of all," continued Hedake, smiling that ziggy-zag smile, "is that a senior representative of the Greenpower Company, which helps businesses explore sustainable alternatives, approached me during yesterday's performance to say that the commitment, enthusiasm and imagination of the children has led him to commit a significant investment to St Aubergine's environmental projects, in collaboration with the Bottomley Car Factory's renewable energy experiments. He wants it to be known that his company wishes these developments to be activated at the earliest opportunity. This is marvellous news for the school, and marvellous news for the factory. Indeed, it is marvellous news for the whole of Bottomley!"

Just as I thought it couldn't get any better, Hedake sunk me with a low blow.

"But there is the question of the nit farm," she said, looking serious.

Quite a large number of the Infants, who had

stuck their heads in the Nitz Hotel, had apparently been scratching like maniacs ever since.

"And you should have realised, Patricia, it wouldn't save the nits, because you know dear, nits suck our blood. They can't live on hair alone, dear. So they will jump OFF the hair in the box and *on* to the hair of the person who is sticking their head in."

WHAT? Nits suck our *blood*?! *Euugh.* I was feeling about nit-high at this point.

My mum and dad had their eyebrows going through the tops of their heads at this moment, but at least their foreheads looked a lot happier.

"Still, perhaps the nicest news of all," trilled Hedake, "is that our dear Ms Mortice is staying as a result of a very happy occurrence."

The "very happy occurrence" was to be the wedding of Warty-Beak and Mortice. Obviously, clinging to him in terror had roused some deep lizardy feelings in his lizardy breast. Or perhaps the sight of her covered in scarlet nail varnish had aroused a distant memory of his own planet, where you probly drank blood at the wedding feast... poor Mortice! She little knew the fate that awaited her!

I gazed at her in pity, but she mistook it for pleasure, I think, because she smiled a smiley smile at me, while Warty-Beak's terrifying mug almost cracked in two.

"Meanwhile," went on the Hedake, "I am writing to the Education Minister to explain that I think it would be an excellent idea if St Aubergine's were to withdraw from the English Primary Exams for next year, so that we can concentrate on some creative writing and contemplation, instead of, as Freddy so astutely put it 'counting adverbs'."

"What about Maths and Science?" I asked, before I could tell my brain to keep my trap shut.

"A step at a time, Patricia," said Hedake in her steely-soft head teacher voice. "Maths and Science are full of facts that are more simple to test and you wouldn't want to go up to secondary school not knowing your times tables, would you?"

Goodness me no, I thought. How Very Extremely sad that would make me. But I just smiled my politest smile and said, "Er, thanks."

"Patricia, you are excluded..." (What? What? What have I done now? Am I hearing right?) "...from any blame. Now please tell Freddy Jones to come in and hurry to your classroom. Oh, and tell Freddy I won't bite his head off, will you?"

YES!!!!

I roared out of the office giving everyone high fives and soon the good news spread.

So now I am back in bed and wondering about a few things. I am wondering about the characters of nits. I mean, are nits NICE? I feel dead daft about the blood sucking. Still they're only little and don't know any better, do they? I mean, they're a lot littler than Tomato, so they must know even less than him, and what he knows could be written on a nit's paw at the best of times.

The Infants' School and the Wigs Within It have now apparently been completely overtaken by nits, thanks to the Nitz Hotel. Maybe I should rethink my relationship with nits.

I am also thinking about Magic.

I think the reason I played my trumpet better than ever was the Magick

Grade Twelve Trumpet book calling to me from my trumpet case. I mean, if it hadn't been for those mushrooms and woodlice dancing, I would've hit that last note just right. And the ghost potion worked too. I know it wasn't a real ghost, but it was just after Grandma Tempest sent me the potions that I discovered the truth. So I bet there is some connection. And anyway Freddy and Eight Brains Eric did all the Green Hand stuff, but what about the skull Dinah saw? And what about the cold wind I felt? I bet it was a bit of a ghost. I bet it was a car worker ghost coming back to do his bit.

I asked Bonzo, who I am very glad to say has taken to sleeping with me ever since last night when I looked a bit sad and Tomato gave me the card. And Bonzo thought it was a bit of a ghost, too.

So there! I am hanging on to that Secondary School Ghost potion, just in case.

Tweenage Tearaway

Trixie Tempest

and The Amazing Talking Dog

by Ros Asquith

Trixie has more on her mind than boy bands and butterfly
tattoos, she's out to Save the World. But first she needs
cash, and fast, before Mum and Dad find out she's lost her
precious trumpet. Enter Harpo, her amazing, talking,
singing, yap-artist dog. Is this hound-with-a-sound
too good to be true? Read and believe!

www.fireandwater.co.uk

An imprint of HarperCollins*Publishers*